By Desire

Sam North is the author of
The Automatic Man, which won the
1990 Somerset Maugham Award for Fiction,
The Gifting Programme and *Chapel Street*.
He lives in London.

SAM NORTH

By Desire

Minerva

A Minerva Paperback
BY DESIRE

First published in Great Britain 1996
by Martin Secker & Warburg Limited
This Minerva edition published 1997
by Mandarin Paperbacks
an imprint of Reed International Books Ltd
Michelin House, 81 Fulham Road, London SW3 6RB
and Auckland, Melbourne, Singapore and Toronto
www.minervabooks.com

A CIP catalogue record for this title
is available from the British Library
ISBN 0 7493 9589 3

Phototypeset in Janson
by Intype London Ltd
Printed and bound in Great Britain
by Cox & Wyman Ltd, Reading, Berkshire

5.45 p.m.

Singer-entertainer-barman Larry Azure is on his way to work so it's one foot in front of the other now and looking up he breathes it all in: the street furniture in various states of disrepair, a general retail commerce fronting passers-by with more or less garish signs offering services, the houses with people's lives going on just the same as his but different, every step of the way human effort, work done by human hands like his own, his job at the pub waiting, the time set, as usual a marker to be aimed at, on the dot will do.

It's the same for millions of others, Larry reminds himself, everyone has to do the work, take the shilling and go home again, it's a circle that has to be trotted round even by a large, shambolic, flat-footed and curly-haired Irishman such as yourself; more's the pity, he silently but emphatically tells everyone sharing the road with him at the moment, because weren't we all free and innocent children, once?

As he rounds the corner into Dill Road he wipes the back of his hand across his mouth because he was moving his lips then, probably talking out loud like a lunatic and now there's a tear in his eye for not much reason.

And there's no doubt, is there, that everyone – him, her, the ones gliding by in the cars – as he does himself, holds two or three thoughts that they turn over and over in their heads to juggle any possible answers to the situations they're in so they can move themselves forward. This Mexican-looking woman here with the bandanna and the thin plastic supermarket bag stretched to breaking will have a decision or two to worry away at, big or small. The short fellow with the countryman's hat on striding along – he looks as though he's made up his mind about something. We're all at it, thinks Larry.

Because sure enough he has a decision of his own to cut and dry here, doesn't he; and he should ask himself is it made, is it iron-cast, does each step tamp it down firm as the tarmac on the road beneath him? The sorriness of it is, surely he's decided the issue already several times but can't stop changing his mind; if it's a Thursday he's thinking yes, if it's a Friday he's saying it's the wrong thing, so any decision he might own up to can't be trusted at all. He grumbles, What a life.

So why then is he bouncing back and forth on the decision – why-oh-why, he hears himself echo the catchphrase?

He knows the answer – because it's a two-paths-dividing-in-the-wood situation which has him scratching his head here at the fork looking down one sunny and dappled pathway as it were, to see his top-notch wife, the one he's pledged to in the eye of God and in his own mind, the one he loves, not to mention maybe a bit further down the same path a batch of children playing at her feet; and yet if he's only to glance down the other path, it's to see all the fucking beautiful, smooth-skinned, fuckable women that might be his to take under his wing for a night or two or longer.

So, it's the wife or the mistress – you can't have both, he tells himself, because the thought of his wife leaving him is a dire one all right; it'd be like a fist reaching into his innards and pulling out his own very happy child-hood, his, Larry's, root and branch, leaving him a broken man as sure as if you'd have taken the engine out of a motor. Yes, that's how it'd be somehow, given his own parents' good marriage and large family back home and the importance of that memory in him, *therefore shall a man leave his father and mother and cleave unto his wife.*

Yet who would be stuck in a sweet shop and promise to walk out empty-handed – point himself only at the baby-mother, as the Rastas have it? Isn't it true, how a new woman can open up a man's existence? The first smile is like a door to a different world suddenly opened with the extra sunshine thrown in for the honeymoon period; but for the sake of the promise, the pledge you've made, the marriage, and the children that are to arrive one day, you're to say no – isn't that a hard climb for everyone, not just him, isn't there a touch of the Mount Everest about it – not messing with other women?

He's been stuck here at this point in the argument long enough to have worn a little hole in the ground walking back and forth to see as far as possible down each pathway, both of them glorious and sunlit and full of promise and satisfaction, what with having such an A1 mistress and a first-class wife as he has, at the moment. He swears, Christ!

He's on the last leg of his walk to work now, crossing by the disused café where he used to have his pools coupon collected and still wondering what the name is of the strange tree which looks like it should be growing out of an African plain but instead is here leaning at a dangerous angle centred on a square of paving stones with the remains of a black plastic sheet caught in its branches. He wonders why this corner is always deserted and has the sense of bad weather, a cloud over it, all the time; perhaps it's the tree that does it.

In a few minutes he'll hit the Crescent where the pub stands and there won't be much time for thinking left so he ought to decide here and now finally with no more back-and-forth.

To give himself a moment or two more, he stops and leans against the corner of the wall. He thinks, It's all about sex, isn't it – and doesn't every single fellow have this visual shape of a woman like a key as it were to unlock their Y-fronts and their cocks all aim in the same direction, towards this mould that they want to do the business with, not concerned with who it is or why or the woman's talk or her character or soul or whatnot. Fill the right measurements – the C-cup and the tiny waist and the full hips – and you can recut the cloth and give the men drinking at the bar of the Dreghorn Castle any woman, any colour or creed and they'd hardly notice or know which one to choose.

More than that, the measurements have a certain direction – how small the waist, how protuberant there and how curved here – which in the *Daily Sport* you might see made a cartoon of, showing girls with waists you can fit a hand around yet pneumatic fronts, somehow, probably through trick photography and airbrushing refinements.

And when he was young, Larry joined in all right, he drooled over the sex clubs and lapped up the porno films; for instance he remembers the one that put the woman into a rubber suit with an inflatable head, that is to say a double-layered mask, the first skin-tight which must have been like wearing a condom, with a valve similar to a bicycle's for the girl to breathe through, then the second layer like a loose bladder into which air was pumped to give her zero personality indeed like a football, the whole outfit as featured in the skin magazines, with the carefully positioned zips to discover her breasts and so on and the valve right there sticking out with a knurled screw at the end to control her breathing, allowing absolute power to the maniac truck driver who was eventually unleashed on her.

That's what he's up against – Christ – the teenager in him. He kicks his toe against the corner.

Decide, Larry, which path?

In his heart he knows what the answer is because it'll be the one that changes everything; he's after being a more sound man from the top down, good, in charge of himself, his socks pulled up and not so round-shouldered, standing square to the world. He has the new job, the life carrying an upward slant and the woman he loves as his wife. He doesn't want to queer it, being the traditional skunk he's always enjoyed being, so.

Therefore what it means it – right to the point as far as he's concerned at the moment – if there's no mistresses allowed, he'll have to chuck Laura.

Laura also is on her way to work, but she's taken a detour and here she is, wandering down the aisle of the chemist's. The music blares from a hidden speaker in the ceiling and is suddenly louder and the words of the song sound like they're coming from under water. A lovely day . . .

Oh very lovely, thinks Laura.

She's looking for nothing she wants exactly – this isn't a fun shopping trip, Life itself is twisting her arm to make her come in here. She cruises the length of the counter, but it's not the deodorants, nor the hairgrips, soaps, nor the dispensary, she's after. The condoms are closer to the mark, she thinks. They're packaged like weird drugs with hippie names like 'Gossamer' and psychedelic patterns printed on the packets – hey, that's what an orgasm looks like?

Next to them, on the same shelf, is the reality: thanks for putting them so close together, don't beat about the bush, will you – these pregnancy testing kits are where that little adventure takes you, make no mistake, she thinks ironically.

Ignoring the two what seem like Asian children in white coats behind the cash till, she stares hard at the different brands: Discover Today, Predictor, Clearblue. She reads the slogans: so simple you can't go wrong; simple, fast, accurate; results in three minutes. All of the packages contain two tests. The prices are the same.

Out of the gaze of the Asian children she can put her duffle bag on the floor for a moment and check her purse.

She takes Discover Today and holds it in her hand. She weighs it: almost nothing, light as paper.

Her horoscope advised her, Step outside yourself, and it will put a sense of distance between you and your troubles.

She thinks, Yes please, as far away as possible. She imagines floating out of her body, higher and higher. Look, there she is, way down there, standing with her head bowed, the blonde hair bell-shaped hanging from the headband and the one hand holding her coat closed over her work-clothes, the other hefting this package. Someone help that girl.

Looking down at this thing she has to buy, so at a crossroads in her life but with all the planets lined up pulling the different energies in the world this way and that, influencing everything as surely as anyone's willpower, she asks herself what's the point in struggling with it, she ought to go with the flow, man.

Hearing the click of a woman's shoes and the more distant burble of the radio she thinks, Look, there's her hand, what's it going to do?

Maybe she'll stay like this until it moves of its own

accord. She's very psychic, isn't she? She knows automatically which page to turn to in the newspaper to find the TV pages so she's more tuned into modern-day vibes than most people.

So right now she opens herself to what the world wants to do with her: come on, world, do your stuff. To help it make up its mind she moves her hand experimentally and then steadies herself waiting, while voices come at her as though from further away, although it's only the woman she heard earlier walking along on her heels being served, probably.

Her hand moves abruptly, offering the cellophane-wrapped package to the boy in the white coat. She can't hang around for ever.

While the boy takes it and drops it into a bag she unclips her purse and retrieves the ten-pound note, meanwhile dabbing at the nervous tic in her eye – she was staring for too long, concentrating. Then she takes her purchase and leaves.

At the doorway, just as she's leaning against the glass with the word 'Push' written on it, a man steps towards her coming from nowhere and says something she can't make out.

She looks round; standing some inches lower than her an older Asian man – maybe the father or even grandfather of the boys behind the till – is raising his eyebrows and repeating the same phrase, which she still can't understand.

Angry with him for being smaller than her and confronting her like this she asks, You what, sorry? in an accusing voice.

Again he's saying something, longer this time, it sounds like an explanation, ending with the numbers, Two one.

She asks, What?

The man's eyebrows are raised high on his forehead and he has one finger pointing at her, his smile saying ... she doesn't know.

Then he's lifting a pair of blank video cassettes bound together in plastic film from a dump-bin that stands at his elbow; she reads the words HIGH RESOLUTION.

The father or grandfather says, One-hundred-twenty minutes, two for the price of one if you want.

Suddenly his words have separated at the right places for her to get it: he's trying to flog her the videos.

Momentarily she relaxes and is surprised how far her shoulders droop suddenly; she must have been puffing herself up like the cat does, sensing danger.

Then she's through the door and away, shaking her head at the sense of everyone missing each other, not under-standing each other's hearts at all; and this is Saint Valen-tine's Day.

Larry Azure is ducking under the red-and-white tape guarding the roadworks and hopping among the broken pavement slabs.

And right now, tonight, even before work starts he'll come out with it and say, Laura, it's over.

Because she and both her legs will be there at the pub as usual.

If he imagines her, it's a view from behind which is telling him, look at the famous egg-timer shape – but isn't it to advise him time has run out all right for suchlike enjoyment?

He knows when he tells her the bad news her eyes will be like pebbles just visible on the bottom of a stream, expressionless but to him inviting, her moods you might say the water passing over them, muddy or not.

Christ, but she's a good class of flesh all right, look how he can't stop himself thinking about it, and the shoulders there, bare knobs at the tops of her arms, are a delight to hold, one in each hand, handles to pull on, the tufts of hair in her pits terrible with scent, her feet waving behind his ears and the tendons in her arms like wires, while she's stringing him along.

Should any man resist having such a mistress? he asks himself, even for the heartburn and suffering and loss it'll mean when it blows him and his wife apart and stops them from having kids; and then he thinks, this isn't the last of it either, her attraction to him, since he and Laura will be meeting every night unless he ditches the job at the pub – which maybe he can do, now he's got the Sunday night slot carved out for himself on Talk Radio and he's halfway to paying back the overdraft.

But the dilemma is, if he's to chuck Laura and the rubber

suit he was momentarily asking her to wear back then, with the buckles exactly how you might like them, according to the aficionados, even down to the type of popper or fastener or zip pull and the exact location of every strap and button, what's the technique, if it's to last for ever as a fully switched-off, copper-bottomed no? If he's to turn from these pictures of rubber dolls containing real human bodies which he wants and can have a bullish sort of fun with, if he's to turn from lust in other words, in order to save the one thing that if he were a soul passing through St Peter's Gate and he was asked what is most heavenly, he'd say must be the serious answer, love itself no less – and he's to turn away from it for ever – what is the fucking technique, the way of doing it?

Cut your own balls off, Larry, is maybe an answer worth looking at.

No, too pricey by half, as a proposition. Leave them out of it, keep your balls firmly to hand, Larry.

So, from beyond the dark sky overhead dragged by jumbo jets and helicopters and other city paraphernalia, he asks for some God-given guidance on how else to stop his hands from heading for Laura's zips and buttons and the hems of her skirts. He wants an easy answer such as change these brown shoes passing back and forth beneath him for black ones and it'll be done, you'll be a changed man.

And don't even think about her bumps, he warns himself, if tonight he's going to try and stop from sliding down the slippery slope so repeatedly as he has been doing. Christ, he's burning to catch sight of her tits even clothed and from a distance, right now, leave alone take her bra-clip in his fingers and free them, the beauties.

With the women, maybe it's like giving up smoking, in which case should he tease himself off Laura by cutting down from four times a week to three to once a week and so on, until it's a small enough step to refrain altogether? Or, might he consider the other way: with a heroic effort say no, never again, and from that moment count it as something you don't do, honest-to-God, life-and-death.

He's been walking along staring at the ground like he was always told not to when he was a boy so when he looks up he's lost momentarily – but it's only because he's gone a few steps beyond his turning so he retraces his steps and finds his way again, after a while seeing the pub itself and approaching with the usual mix of dread and excitement as each stride carries him nearer to the music and the audience and the booze and the money as usual, but in addition tonight the confrontation with Laura.

The Dreghorn Castle public house stands foursquare and optimistic on this bedevilled corner of the city, all glad signwork and boasting the mural of a snooker player, the washed paint and polished glass with the curtains matching in colour and design and neatly run across on poles – all this struggling against the scene outside, the grey pavements overcast by the orange and purple night sky and the lighted casements and shop doorways square-shouldered and facing each other across the Crescent and the graffiti on the wall opposite the pub and the smell of the street washed clear of debris after the market and the abandoned furniture pulled apart by kids and wetted by rain, lying there casually behind the railings where the dogs go, invariably.

Arriving at this spot, Larry consults his watch and he's here more than a touch early, it's a choice between dawdling in the street outside or going in through the double doors and wasting his own good time in there; the *thwump* as they close behind him is always a reminder he won't be out much before midnight probably although he'll be hearing the swinging back and forth all night, people coming, then leaving, making their way to and from the piles of flats that are set down hereabouts like space-stations, dwarfing the idiotic cars and streets and houses and buzzing with noise from some points, other bits silent and as though unoccupied, but the giant steel garbage sheds at the bottom of them full to bursting and so indicating the measure of human appetite within, all right.

There's a quarter of an hour before his official start-time so more than that, half an hour or so, for his own use because he's normally a bit late with no questions asked, nowadays, due to his wee measure of fame on the radio and that bringing a new face or two into the place, spending money.

For a moment he dawdles with his back to the Dreghorn Castle, hands in pockets.

He checks his watch a time or two and taps it with the long nail on his right-hand index finger which he uses to pick at his guitar with.

He tugs at a sprig of hair and it bounces back quick as ever; it'll take a shock all right to uncurl it, his hair.

The first time he put his hand on Laura's stomach, if he remembers rightly, it was that time he was pressing her against the pool table – and sneaking his hand under her skirt it was soft as a pat of butter laid from hip to hip. She wanted to do the sit-ups and make it flat as a model's; he told her not to.

Is she inside the pub there already, or not?

He wonders why he started out from home so early and answers himself, maybe he was bored and needed to be out seeing things and people passing by, to be sniffing around like the blessed dogs, but more probably it's this struggle going on, he has to be out of the house, away from his wife, to think clearly what to do and now he has the answer: he has to face up to it and say no to the mistresses, for evermore, starting tonight with Laura who may or may not be behind those swing doors yet, but for sure she will be later on.

Certainly he's not one to turn up for work early. What would that do for the reputation of a singer-entertainer-barman? He'd be dead in the water if it got out.

But he shouldn't lurk about the place like a teenager, either. Buck up, he tells himself, though he wouldn't mind somehow getting to watch Laura's arrival, her prodding the door open, her loping walk while shrugging out of an overcoat and her immediately sitting at one of the wee tables to recover with a cigarette, the Landlord's beady eye on his prize barmaid all the while – if he gets an early sight of her then he can judge her mood, so when and how exactly he should duck in and deliver the knock-out blow, give her the bad news.

Or he could go off for a dander around the area and forget about Laura, out of sight is out of mind, so he can relax, get his head straight, focus – then when she does swim into view he'll know what to do and how.

Starting off down this side of the Crescent he tells himself, think about it, yes, how will he put the stoppers on it, as an affair? What's the strategy?

The best way is, he'll just say no to her any which way it comes, without working out the politics of doing it in advance at all.

Then he has this question which pops up in his mind as unexpectedly as a target in a fairground shooting gallery: has he ever seen Laura outside the four walls of the Dreghorn Castle public house?

He's stopped in his tracks by this because it's weird, isn't it – having an affair with her but his never seeing her in the light of day, or in real life at all? Why's he never crossed with her even coming from the bus stop or whichever?

He walks on more slowly. The cries of the Asian youths bantering outside the paper shop slide by him.

Has he walked down a street with her or sat in the takeaway waiting for an order, or shared a cab even? Not one bit. He sees various characters here outside he recognises but will probably never know to talk to – the Chinese takeaway delivery boy outside with his moped levered on its stand there and his helmet perched at the back of his head, and the fruit and veg. man tightening the straps on his trolley – but never Laura.

So does she arrive by magic then, conjured on the doorstep as it were, a genie to rub him up the right way like the booze itself and as dangerous?

Think of it like that, he tells himself – with her as a witch or a manifestation of some type, a ghost, a devilish appearance and temptation to himself, Larry Azure, an illusion real enough to touch, yes, and to get to the inside of like she was any other mistress, but guess what, the proof she's an image in his head only is, she can't be seen outside the swing doors here, instead disappearing into thin air; it's like in the vampire movies when the creature looks in the mirror and there's no reflection.

And how can you shape up and grapple with such a thing, he asks himself, it's impossible.

Dream on, Larry, he tells himself, there isn't such an easy way to get rid of the problem; a snap of his fingers and a shake of a magic wand won't do the trick at all. He'll find out later sure enough that inside the province of the pub, Christ, she'll be convincing all right: there'll be her cigarette parked on the lip of the ashtray and the vodka and orange only sipped and having apparently no effect on her behaviour, and her duffle bag at her feet, these personal items somehow more important than anybody else's, perhaps because there's a sort of royalty in having a cleavage like hers which as well allows her the quiet and staring manner she has; she knows everyone will be looking at her, and on top of that she has her high-heeled walk that says,

Hey, I'm fun, I know what I'm doing and look here, feel the heat coming off me – all of this is one hundred per cent real, Larry, you can't go round playing at my being a ghost.

He thinks, She's a delicate thing, habitual, serious – but awesome to the drinkers who view her like tourists from a distance. They've not seen much better than her outside of magazines and so they're not sure of themselves, they're shy, because the Dreghorn Castle is a haven for astray souls, so, normal in that tradition of public house life.

He realises then, what he's looking at through the shop glass is a set of Valentine's cards at least two foot square in size and quilted for extra luxury to impress whichever loved one is to receive it and it's the fourteenth this very day. Christ how the world is obvious and smacks you in the face, Larry thinks; again it's like in those same vampire movies when the thunder cracks and lightning strikes over the heads of the characters and you think, why shouldn't it be a sunny day for God's sake when the guy gets out of the grave and bites people. He reads some of the messages in the cards which go, Thank You For Caring, or, Loving You Is Beautiful; it's no help to his choosing the right moment to jump one way or the other, that kind of syrup coming at him.

Leaving his reflection in the glass he pushes his hands deeper into his pockets and faces into the wind with his elbows well tucked into his sides for more warmth. He strolls past the chippie where he goes often enough to know the girl serving is called Veronica because it's written

in gold around her neck; it'll be dead warm in there which
would be nice but he carries on and bypasses the post office
with its metal front shuttered; outside the corner shop he
turns his back to the wind, the litter scattering past him
daintily, and he looks up at the flats, layers of them six
high, wondering who exactly is within switching the lights
on and off, and more especially where the drinkers live
who'll come later to listen to his singing, and also where
the criminals are hiding who break into these shops so
often, even the chemist's and the doctor's for the drugs
now so they've fortified their premises, concreting in the
back windows and adding to the Beirut atmosphere here
although there's not much bodily violence and the people
are cheery in the shops always; and all these shenanigans are
talking-points among the drinkers in the Dreghorn Castle
on any given evening. Larry thinks, they were all children
once, wanted and loved by their parents most of them,
more or less.

He looks up the main road and ponders where the pub's
territory ends, what's the furthest anyone has to stagger
home; it's probably not much beyond this corner here, yet
there's many within the boundary of the Crescent and the
road at the end who won't ever set foot in the Dreghorn
Castle and so haven't ever heard him; these Pakistanis in
the corner shop for instance, they're missing out – and
how – without Larry Azure at night to cheer them up. Do
they know it even, though? Tune in to 1053 kHz, one
o'clock, Sunday night, he tells them. Seeing the spectacled
face of the shop-owner look up from the till to catch his

eye through the glass and aluminium door bedecked by sales posters Larry silently asks him, come along tonight why don't you? At the same time he registers the insults daubed in black paint on the chipboard covering a broken window and he recognises this is what keeps them from going into the pub; if he were a photographer instead of a singer-entertainer-barman that's when he should have clicked the shutter: that elderly Asian face paled by the London winters, next to it the slogans promising racial attack. Material for the show, he thinks, tuck it away Larry and do a spot of anti-racism.

Did Laura just go in here and buy cigarettes, handing over the coins but angry at the tax on them going up and up, emptying the little oval-shaped purse she has with the clip on the top, walking back to the pub over this exact spot?

Come Sunday night and he's at Talk Radio, the microphone a heavy, fat prong hanging in front of him, the antennae on the roof broadcasting away up there, the scene he's to have with Laura tonight will be over; however bad it's going to be will have been soothed by a couple of days of subsequent goings-on and generally stitched into his past along with all the other colourful happenings. He'll cheerfully warn the men among his audience, watch out for the women, maybe they're like a gaudy curtain which you have to barge through at a certain time of your life in order to get the other side of them and have more of a hold on yourself. If you're captivated by the colour of the curtain and the way it moves and you sit there entranced and so on, you're done for. So he'd suggest, go for it, run anyhow and plunge through it and live with what it brings you, whether that's boredom or not, but in any case watch closely what it does to your souls and remember, *give not thyself over to a light woman*. Write to me for help and advice as well as to let me know what happens; I'll always take a telephone call, first come first served.

As for the ladies and what notional metaphor or message would be useful for them, he might ask his audience, you tell me. Is a woman's lust for men the same, there?

Larry walks back towards the Dreghorn Castle on the other side of the road in order to look into different darkened shopfronts, the wind on his back now, his longish hair tickling both cheeks because it's blown forward.

He's charging himself up to tell Laura no, he's sorry but it's over, tonight he's going to better himself, maybe it's a first step towards having kids; and he pictures the restful place beyond, when it's all done, his wife illuminated as she would be in his eyes by the sort of light that's talked about on the north-western coast of Ireland, gentle, serene, open and long-lasting.

Finding himself standing on the opposite side of the road from the pub he checks his watch and finds he should be starting work now by rights.

It's appreciably darker, perhaps because of the broken streetlight here outside the Chinese takeaway. He looks around him, for a while.

The double doors to the Dreghorn Castle stand there, unmoving.

She just walked over this kerbstone, he imagines. The street was crossed by her shadow. The prick of her heels landed here, there . . .

Christ, it's all very well in theory but she's a flesh and blood woman; who knows what'll happen.

So he takes extra licence as he can nowadays and decides for a takeaway (and he can eat the Dreghorn Castle's sandwiches later).

Going into the Chinese, Larry asks his metaphorical listeners, How many of you guys is it, that get on the outside of a fast-food portion on a Friday night as a comfort or substitute for not having Lauras of your own? Many millions it must be and I'm about to join you voluntarily, can you believe it?

In here they're queuing for the meals that have numbers, like betting prospects. 32 with 8 is his choice; ordering it numerically is like something out of science fiction, it strikes him.

Taking a slot on the wooden bench to wait for his order he's among a handful of other gentlemen and he reminds himself they've all got a pair of balls exactly the same as him, and looking downwards he gives his own a quick talking to, saying, maybe it'll be disappointing from now on, we're chucking out the chance of any amount of great-looking and young mistresses that might be enjoyed in the entire number of future years left to us – and for the sake of Christ it's a sacrifice.

He remembers their first meeting, his and Laura's, when she asked whether it was his real name, Larry Azure; it was

an evening shift at the Dreghorn Castle and back then he
wasn't doing the barwork as well, he was only the singer
twice a week on various days and he asked her back, was
she joking, using your real name in this business isn't trying
hard enough or having the sort of fun an offbeat singer-
entertainer is meant to have, by tradition now, thanks to
Tutti Frutti showing twice on the television. Her response,
which was mostly just this listening, the level gaze she has
that might mean nothing or everything, made him continue
on with the story – that when he was first looking for a
stage name he favoured the single words like Sting or Ice,
he judged them the most memorable and he went looking
for an anti-heroic version of the same thing, and he was
going to call himself Grub.

Grub? she asked in her flat kind of voice and he
answered, yes because it suited his grainy skin and sloping
shoulders and the general softness of his physique.

And despite his admitting he was a touch overweight she
was still there in front of him like a willing victim which
excited him a wee bit, her invitation to come on, to continue, so he did, when she asked him how did he come
across this particular name Larry Azure?

His answer was, there was this character called Larry
Azure for real.

Whereabouts? she asked after a long enough silence, and
he said, it was this fellow selling car and home insurance
around the estate I live in, sort of a short and balding
fellow, yet people bought off him because of his name, it
sold him, she should have seen the Mercedes 190 car he

turned up in, people were under his spell, to be called Larry Azure is rich and famous already.

Then it was, so, when her first smile came, a little thing at the corner of her lips which he knew was the start of it.

She asked is that what he was after, fame and money, and he said he was, so he snitched the name, maybe he'd have his own Mercedes before long. Dream on, she'd replied, or something like that, but she was listening to him steadily after giving him that smile, the hard gaze she has not leaving him, that was how she got under his skin, just by allowing him to soak her up for long enough, so canny, a woman's way right enough.

She asked what it was like to have someone else's name and he admitted that at first it was uncomfortable, like an overly new leather jacket which wears its owner instead of vice versa, but now, having called himself Larry Azure for four years it's his own name that's strange, an old friend who might embarrass him, no less.

Then she gave her second wee play at being interested, not a smile this time but a serious look it was which told him this wouldn't be nothing, no sir.

Christ, he's to shake himself by the scruff of the neck and get the other side of Laura, to the end of it; tonight or never, he tells himself. After all he's on the verge of glory, and given his radio career carries on beyond the single late-late-night slot a week there'll be any amount of Lauras on tap – look at Caesar the Geezer or Jeremy Beadle and how they turn on to those two – and if he can't say no to a Laura now, how then will he fight off the multitude

when success cuts in for real; he'll have to check himself
into a sex clinic like Michael Douglas did and one for the
drink as well most likely – he'll be stumbling from one
establishment to the other and back like Barrymore, Liz
Taylor and the rest of them. Then, suddenly cheerful at
the thought of that he shakes his head and asks, Please for
God's sake can that be the only price of his upcoming
fame, he might expect worse than such lunatic behaviour
bubbling inside him due to the money and the adoration
– it'll be doubly sad for instance if people in general suddenly treat him differently because he's famous and so he'll
lose his touch because what he needs is to slope around
the streets and pause for a while here and there and belong,
be part of things, which a famous person is stopped from
doing. Hopefully if it's just his voice that's recognisable he
can prevent that. He won't allow press photographs to
appear so his face will be unknown. He imagines holding
up a hand and saying just that, No photos please.

Now his number's called by the oriental sweetheart and
up he goes to take the bag from the counter and he catches
a sideways glimpse of the newspaper which the gingery
fellow is reading; of course there's a girl with her kit off
right there on page three, the familiar double loop across
the chest complete with a smile on the girl's face for the
boys – *look not round about thee in the streets of the city*.

Threading back through the queue, he looks out of the
glass shopfront and sees the Dreghorn Castle framed and
lit like it's a picture and not a window at all, and the sudden
shiver of alarm at the thought of Laura flying at him when

she hears the bad news has him funnily enough deciding to stay and eat the meal in here just for a moment or two more's peace so when he shoulders through the mill of people just coming in through the door bringing a blast of the cold outside air as well as a black and white dog which is then turned on and shouted at to go outside and sit and stay, he can take his place on the bench again ready to eat, but he finds he's not hungry at all – instead of hunger it must be a pang of nerves so it is, considering his fate this evening.

Mind you he'll still force it down so as not to be wasting money entirely and it'll mean he'll be less drunk by the end of play tonight, hopefully, although there'll be every reason to drink himself senseless, to celebrate the victory over the Lauras.

So, starting on the beef-and-ginger with the flat wooden fork, he's summing up the three gentlemen and one lady waiting for their meals here in the Chinese takeaway and he thinks, Not only were we all babies once, but all of us still are just that; a mother plied that gingery fellow with milk like he was the bee's knees which is a strange thought when here he is scratching his bollocks and leafing through the paper on the counter there with his torn pocket hanging off his jeans, but guess what it is he's queuing for, it's food isn't it, the same as he cried for back then, and he'll be wanting love and attention afterwards and then some entertainment. The only difference is, everything's more difficult for him now he's to find these things for himself.

Making an imaginary broadcast about the Laura situation

– he has this habit of thinking about possible material for his show as he moseys around during the week – he would begin in his famed conversational tone, Listeners, for Chrissakes, what is it about Laura, her measurements mostly, that are, well, let's say so fucking tempting to us *fuck-fuck* gentlemen. I think I know the answer already, but someone please call in tell me I'm right, how can thirty-six C-cup inches of youthful and rounded breast tipped with a perfect nipple, twenty-seven inches of waist with that dot of the naval a marker to tell you how far you've got left to go, rising to thirty-six of hip, the circle of it yours and my handle like a fucking steering wheel, gents, to drive into her with and then falling by thirty-two die-straight inches of walking, running, crossed or uncrossed inside leg, for the sake of Christ, with stockings on or bare flesh in summer with a light tan, then on top of that regular features like the nose above the mouth and the teeth straight and hair that length and so on which is a pattern, no more nor less – how can that simple equation such as you might have learnt in a maths class at school cause such ongoing havoc in the bar of the Dreghorn Castle? I ask you, are we machines gone haywire?

And he'd have the coffee there to hand and the earphones covering one ear and the glass screen in front of him through which a cheerful live artist awaits his or her cue, visible through his own reflection while he's adding, By the way a big hello to Laura who's working at the Dreghorn Castle seven shifts a week where I'm lucky enough to do a weekend spot myself and forgive me for giving your personal measurements over the air, Laura, especially having myself given you the push in no uncertain manner there, the night before last, but then also, isn't it half decent of me not to give everyone your phone number and tell them the tricks you know with your hands?

Larry shakes his head at the crime he's about to commit tonight against her person. No wonder he's delaying here with his beef and ginger and the chip he's not at all hungry for.

Catch yourself on, we're not machines at all, Larry corrects himself, but animals. The sight of a woman and we're real dogs, aren't we; in fact if he recalls the four or five mongrel strays that hang around his neighbour's doorway when the wee bull terrier called Skylark is on heat, all moping about in a sort of queue or pecking order and fighting among each other, then even those dogs' faces bear a resemblance to the expressions of the men queuing here in the Chinese.

So if men are dogs first and human beings afterwards, it's what he's going to have to change, the order of that, and become a human being with the dog tied up out the back starved and forgotten hopefully; so he tells himself, stop sniffing around, can the mistress.

Number 32 with 8 is done for, he's prodded it to death with the wooden fork now lying in the bottom of the foil container there.

Since he's later than ever for work, will they have phoned someone else to take his place?

Relax, Larry, mind the food going down and make your

way slowly over, your fate's sealed; it's something to be faced; no way out.

He stands up, full to his boots with dread, not to mention the two dinners, but finally he's on the last leg.

With the packaging from his meal a nuisance in his hand for now, he lifts his free arm to pass through the swing door of the Chinese out into the street. The palm raised like that may as well be a signal for her, a no-thank-you, there. Larry tells himself, give Laura the push tonight and it'll be a victory and you can be the man you want to be. You walk in that bar tonight on all fours, a dog Larry, but leave at the end of your shift on your hind legs, grown up.

After all, it's Saint Valentine's Day and behind all the business to do with the cards and the roses and the chocolates there must be some deep-rooted myth or suchlike, even more scratched in than the Christian one, which has become embedded in the hearts of us, Larry thinks, so why not tap into the energy, the pattern of that and set himself on the right path tonight.

He folds the aluminium carton and inserts it into the paper bag which held his chip, then dumps the lot in the bin provided outside the Chinese to encourage the young people to behave themselves with the litter.

He wipes his hands on his trousers.

He swipes a curl of hair from in front of his eye.

It's clocking-on time.

The Dreghorn Castle awaits, a safe station for the thirsty and for those requiring spiritual refreshment, if they have the money.

As he crosses the road towards the pub Larry finds his radio-show voice spooling on in his head, he's thinking, this is the moment, ladies and gentlemen, when an ordinary decision has – yes – been made in the life of an ordinary man but nevertheless it should be marked, the peg put in the ground here – it's where he decided to bounce the mistress and go straight, not as harsh as the choices made by many in whatever quarter of the world but to him, Larry Azure, disc jockey, singer, entertainer, star of Talk Radio's one-off Sunday-night slot, it's a killer, he can't say cheerio to the women like he has without crying into his cups and mourning his lost innocence, you might say, as a general, all-round dog with its tail wagging in an uncompli-cated fashion and nothing more than its own hunger to work for.

He's itching to tell everyone about it, to examine with the help and advice of his fellow men his predicament and to hear others' stories and to listen to music which is melancholy enough to fit the occasion.

From here he can see the Day-Glo green poster which he knows has his name on it standing among others in the pub window. He's already told his new radio audience – at the last count thirty-odd thousand, all good souls and hearts of whatever creed or political persuasion – that any sum total of happiness in his life has to include the regular Friday- and Saturday-night gigs here at the Dreghorn Castle, his name, Larry Azure, on the window next to the swing door for passers-by to see for the last two years, off and on, not up in lights exactly but in felt tip, a small-time, you might say low-tech fame, but among good folk, many of whom he knows personally, especially since he's worked there as a barman for another three nights each week for a while, so he's had the building society not quite so much on his back – and he hopes some of his listeners will come down and try him out down here as well, in the flesh.

Work, Larry thinks, equals hours of sweat and the money at the end of it means safety from the wolves at our doors and food in our mouths – so it's no surprise how everyone has to grub for it: himself, the Landlord, Laura, every drinker in the place.

He has this particular way of leaning his back against the door to push it open, meanwhile lifting one foot to tap the bottom corner which snags against the step, turning then, to face up to work it might be said, as he walks into the public bar, all this so he can keep his hands in his pockets.

Here it is, the Dreghorn Castle with its clusters of overhead lights shaped like onions, its flock wallpaper and the jukebox and the Pink Panther gaming machine luring customers with the flashing symbols, the TV a mute, darkened box fixed high on the wall, the cubbyhole for the pool table so cramped that one of the cues is sawn in half to allow shots from the sides where the walls are at your elbow, the L-shaped bar behind which Larry will serve, and the podium there in the corner which is his other arena, where he'll step up to give his performance later on – all this stands as every night, waiting for him. Another, larger poster is there proclaiming, 'Friday and Saturday Nite:

Larry Azure, London's finest DJ and songster, live on stage.'

He sucks in his stomach and tells himself, Go.

As Larry's on his way in, Laura is thumping the door with the mirrored panel in it – which since '94 has been covered with a picture of the Ireland football squad – on her way to the back, so it's a farcical game of in-and-out, doors opening and closing – they don't immediately get to face up to each other.

She has a date with the cardboard box she bought earlier at the chemist's.

She remembers reading, Venus the planet of love moves into the area of your chart that is associated with sex and will stay there for most of February. Which is true enough, it's turning out – how wonderful to be in tune with the cosmos.

The corridor here is painted brown from decades ago, she'd guess. It's not just the dirt sticking to the walls but the smell of stale beer which is like an acid, not the morning-after smell in the bar. The carpet's rotten underfoot. While the pub itself has been done up a few times, who would bother out here. Like men, she thinks, nasty once you reach the back of them.

The sprung doorway to her left leads to the cellar where all the nonsense you need to run a pub is stored; she should be going down the steps here to fetch the decorations for the Valentine's night party but she's on a different tack, this isn't pub business, it's personal.

So at this point it was chosen she should do it . . . she checks her watch and marks the time, the date: it's twenty to seven on the . . . then the breath hisses between her teeth – she hadn't clicked, it's Friday the thirteenth, very bad luck . . .

Then she breathes again. It's Friday the fourteenth, of course.

She thinks of Mystic Meg's voice saying, Now.

And Larry can fetch the *effing* stuff himself when he arrives, why not. It's time he lifted a finger to make a living, he's getting bigger in his boots every day.

Instead, she's to visit her bag, hanging further down the corridor in the cubbyhole to the left.

From this side it would let out to the street if the doorway at the end was in use, but it's been blocked off and the space used to hang coats and store cleaning equipment. Underneath her own leather coat and her duffle bag, the bulk of the clothes have been here for so long they look dead, so unlived in.

Her own coat is new enough and still warm from when she came in compared to the others.

She watches her fingers working at the rope of her bag – nice bag, Laura, she tells herself, you got that right at least – the voice then telling her to take out the kit and get on with it. Delaying has already made things worse in her head. Thinking about it is building up pressure, she recognises the feeling.

D'you want to come and watch, Larry? she asks silently.

Ten bloody quid, to find out if you're pregnant; it's a waste of money if the answer's no and it's worse maybe if the answer's yes – there's the shit-point in taking a test unless you want a kid.

She takes Discover Today and hides it up her sleeve in case anyone should come through the door and surprise her.

She looks down and sees her two feet moving back and forth to carry her to the lav at the end, guess what. Well done, Laura.

These white tiles. Remember it in here, Larry? she asks, sliding the rickety little bolt behind her, all our fucking, quick as monkeys? Well maybe you'd like to see the other side of the coin, it's the pay-off now. Great.

She sits unwrapping the oblong package. With its cellophane skin and the pull-tab, it reminds her of a carton of cigarettes, which is what she wishes it were, but then she thinks, it's shaped more like a cigar, a squared-off Panatella.

The Gemini book said for this month, You may be strongly drawn towards water now, so take a visit to any local beauty spot close to water. You and your lover will find it spiritually refreshing.

Right you are then, here she is at the local beauty spot.

What kind of health warning would you put on a pregnancy test – Babies Can Damage Your Health?

She should know. Let a man near you and they're serious, the after-effects, caused just by lifting her little finger.

Why does it have to be a phallic shape, like everything,

every lipstick, perfume bottle, pint glass, the handle of the
toilet door she opened just now: like men's pricks; even
the ball you hang on to in the tube train on the end of its
little steel wippy-willy type thing is obviously designed by
men to put their little bollocks-shaped ideas in women's
minds.

Talk about obsessive, is she or what.

Her blonde hair hangs on either side, some privacy, a
curtain of hair, not much, is it?

Larry, she thinks, don't mess about telling a girl who's
had an abortion already that you're thinking of having kids
with your wife and that might mean shutting the door on
her, don't say it twice and open the door and close the
door and open it again, her standing there and taking it,
this sort of treatment, for nigh on a year now, and then
the following week go on about your own fucking child-
hood again for the umpteenth time, don't do that and
expect nothing to happen, Larry.

It might have looked like nothing, her reaction all the
time to him, she didn't say a word after all, she listened,
she pretended to have no worries, not to be mad at him;
and sitting here now she can rail on and hate him all she
wants of course but what's the good? Because it's not the
result of love, what's maybe growing inside her. If she'd
had that, her fate might be different, she might have been
taken the distance.

Should she tell him about it, if the plastic tube she's
holding here with the chemistry set inside shows it's true?
Larry, we're having a baby – she can see his face falling.

No, it sure isn't the result of love. The whole thing feels like a biology lesson from school; the signal she gives off is like flowers attracting bees – everyone come and look. No – buzz off. Because no one wants her, not underneath. They only want to see; she feels like a walking accident. Everyone ogling. An accident that you can become involved in. Get yourself hurt. Always at the middle of the accident, is her, injured. Shoo away the onlookers and haul off the others who are involved and there she is on the ground, well battered. So it's protection she needs. Difficult when the display is so strong, like a smell she has.

So that's why, often during sex recently, it's as though she's a frog pinned down in the biology class, her knees open and her arms outstretched and her reproductive organs on display, someone poking about to see how they work.

It's all reproduction, that's what's in her head because of what happened the first time in that clinic, and the fear and the guilt afterwards.

Isn't it all her fault, she reminds herself – from the first mistake comes the second now, maybe, if she is positive.

Inside the Discover Today package she finds two of them, which is another trick. Why not sell them in singles and halve the price? The answer is, they cost nothing to make and the aim is to rake as much money off a person as possible while they're stuck answering the emergency.

She pegs the stick between her knees, at the ready. Leaning over it, she finds herself praying for an all-clear. *Some-*

thing important is happening in your solar seventh house of partnerships . . .

It's routine, you might say; from before she remembers it, the pee not coming despite her bursting for one, it being held in because of nerves. Relax, enjoy yourself, it should say on the instructions.

Also, she can remember walking into the therapist's, on the National Health. There was the room with files and a desk and a phone, like in a set on TV, pot plant and all, it was so ordinary, she was ashamed of being there. There was this woman with the floppy sort of tie at the neck of her blouse, not taking her place on the other side of the desk on purpose, but pulling up a chair next to Laura, to be her friend. She'd smelt of perfume and was middle-aged; what could she know about real life? She'd said, I'm going to say something hard. And it was, it floored Laura and made her realise she was just one of thousands of dumb girls the woman was seeing and saying the same thing to, words she'd been trained to deliver like this, with the warning beforehand. What you might do for the best, the lady said, looking at her intently, is admit to yourself that you're killing your own baby.

Laura had begun to say, You're joking, but she was interrupted, the lady riding over her to add, Because . . . it's what you will tell yourself afterwards.

For the first time then Laura had seen it as a baby with a face and arms waving and about to be killed or not, depending on her making this decision. She saw what the therapist meant, i.e. if you told yourself you were killing it beforehand you might come out the other side of the abortion knowing it was your choice and you were in control of what you were doing, without it backfiring, without it being a surprise that you feel guilty.

She grips the end of the tester and opens her knees, resenting the fiddle. Being a woman, aren't there enough sticks going between your legs of one sort or another; and the mess – women have to clean up spermatozoa and blood and now there'll be pee all over the shop – but it's like holding this magic wand beneath her.

You may be strongly drawn to water now . . . those words ring very true. She's refusing to let go of it.

She does want to delve more into the aspects and their astrological meanings, though. Today is Moon opposite Mercury.

Larry, will you ever know about this? she asks.

Even if he has turned up at last, he'll be out there pussy footing around the bar avoiding any actual work; maybe he's wondering where she is. He can fuck off for ever as far as she's concerned.

Yet, she can expect his soft tap-tap-tap on the door at any moment.

Her nerves jump at the thought.

The leggings are around her ankles and her left elbow's digging into her thigh as the other hand does its job, the mirror opposite her hanging by the one screw drilled into the white tiles showing only the cistern above her head from here – will she remember this and say it's the moment she first knew she was pregnant for the second time? To imagine another kid inside her is like in a movie, like in *Alien* 2 and 3 and so on, the thing lurking yet again, a team of people trying to kill it off, it becoming larger, slippery as the rubber puppet they made for the movie – all blood and guts it is really and growing.

That's it – she's on her way and mixed with the pee diddling in the pan is a chemical produced by her, or something, saying she's pregnant or not, perhaps turning the tester positive with its blue line saying definitely yes or leaving it blank – no.

She could wish for all the eggs in her *fucking* ovaries to be put on hold so she needn't feel like she's in the TV programme she saw on Sunday; women carrying eggs about and dropping one off every four weeks whether they like it or not she knew about of course, who didn't, but she didn't realise she's had the stash of eggs in her from the very beginning, from when she herself was in the womb, for God's sake, so this gobbet of flesh she's tickling for at the moment, if it's a girl, has the next line-up inside her already. The idea makes her feel like she's only a queue of other people all waiting to happen, just luck which one of them shows up, and she's making the next queue now maybe and the responsibility's hard to bear, the lottery of it; suddenly she knows for certain that fate is that much in control, it's choosing one way or the other all the time.

There's silence and the discomfort of her arm between her legs.

She'll only wash one of her hands and use the other to slap Larry's face.

Finished, she withdraws the instrument part way, knocks it against the inside edge of the seat and waits a tick.

The instructions – not that she's had to look at them – say to watch for a blue line to appear in the middle of the Perspex window, but as she lifts the tester and starts the short but important vigil she has this sarcastic thought, Why a line, why not make it a whole picture, a baby's face with its mouth open, crying, that appears.

She waits.

Here we go, Larry, she thinks, maybe you're a father and great, she can be a murderer for a second time. Boil it down and love is no more than a prick coming towards you. Grab it and hang on; you may as well.

Larry's taking a moment to breathe the place in, because Laura's not here; she's usually having a restful vodka and orange and a cigarette to calm down after the trauma of public transport, sitting cross-legged on a stool, one of her shoes part-way off, just hanging from her toe, or in this weather she might be wearing boots, but tonight there's only the Landlord there who's counting at the till, his mouth moving silently, his expression greeting Larry and signalling he shouldn't be distracted.

When he's finished, he drifts behind the bar, slowly and smoothly with his head fixed sideways to count the optics; it gives the impression he's on wheels. He's a good man, pleased with himself and for some good reasons maybe, certainly his humming of ditties must be a sign of content.

Now he can give his usual greeting to Larry, Matey.

Hi-yo, Landlord.

This title, Landlord, is what Larry calls Ray out of respect because the Castle is one of the few remaining free houses working outside the breweries' monopoly, and this heavyweight real-ale fanatic deserves an extra point or two on life's scoreboard because last year he was tied up at knife-point and cut on his face, neck and abdomen while refusing to give the combination to the safe. He was in the papers, his round face smiling and carefree in the photo, not like the battered figure Larry visited in hospital. There is no safe, he kept telling them.

But it's unspoken: even though Laura isn't here right now, Larry and Ray are under starter's orders for the competition they run every night, not to make Laura smile exactly, which would be a hard task, but to win her attention.

Larry hopes, truly, that the Landlord doesn't know how far behind he is. Put a pint of bitter in his hand or give him a set of darts or a pool cue and watch him play and he's an enviable man, having a grace about him, especially charming at the darts when the fix of his eyes gives him a certain direction and sharpness he mightn't otherwise have, and then also, if you watch TV in his company he has a ready humour and a knowledge and a quickness at opening a beercan and catching the froth in his mouth before it spills. Yet, face him with any woman – not just Laura –

and he loses ground, a wrong note comes into his voice which shows up a kind of failure with the gentler sex; Larry guesses the Landlord's ashamed of himself, of his being too heavy and having a soft face and no glamour to him which after all he can see is true, it's in his bathroom mirror night and day, so in the eyes of the women it's equally obvious, his sudden lack of confidence.

On the flip side, it's what gives the Landlord his innocent look, which is what must have charmed his wife into marrying; she would have wanted to look after him. She was the one to work here before Laura; now she's retired upstairs and isn't seen much due to her problem, but Larry thinks of her as a ghost, the spirit of drink itself brooding upstairs, not happy, Ray still down here meanwhile farming away at the alcohol, ploughing the mixed furrow of sadness and gaiety that is the business here in the Dreghorn Castle.

The wall area around Larry's performance podium is bare; there aren't the Saint Valentine's Day decorations up as yet.

Will Laura be fetching them out, is that where she is?

Larry asks, Is Laura in?

Yup.

The Landlord must have been reading his mind because he calls towards the back, Laura!

There's no reply so he shouts louder; then both men hear her smoky voice reply, What?

Ray asks, You got the shagging heart?

What?

He asks again, smiling, The heart, where is it?

The Landlord listens to the silence for a while and then turns away, giving a shrug as he catches Larry's eye.

It's dusted off every year for this night of 14 February, a polystyrene symbol in pink which stands chest-high. There are photos of the Landlord with a different woman around his neck for each of the last few years, taken at the point when the winner of the Lovers' Raffle is announced, and behind them – Ray smiling and the winning woman holding the spirits bottle which is always the prize – is this heart hanging on the wall, daft enough, agreed: with it filling the background of the photograph it's like putting the two poor mortals on the set of a TV game show. God knows when the monstrosity was made but it's comparably flamboyant to certain of the Castle's other fittings, for instance the wallpaper behind the bar is of a nobbly type in metallic gold giving the impression you're working away here on the inside of a beaten copper saucepan and there's a life-size cutout of a girl in a bikini carrying a card with 'Kodak' printed on it which the Landlord took out of the skip when they were clearing out the chemist's over the road, bringing it back to stand in the corner there by the payphone.

Is this the place where the transformation will happen, Larry wonders, and he'll make the first step towards being a sound man top to toe – is this the arena?

And he wonders how the row between him and Laura will be marked out in terms of geography – where should he start it and then whereabouts will it go on? It's not exactly Wembley Stadium here, but it'll be crowded with an audience all right; moreover, he should say the drinkers and listeners and gossip-mongers who gather in here will be actors in the drama also, with more or less big parts to play in the row, no doubt some of them making their own entrances and exits with bits of advice, some disapproving of his bad treatment of the barmaid and what have you while others will be ignorant of what's going on, they'll only see the bits and pieces in between the row like the pulling pints and the singing and the raffle which'll seem more or less normal to them, part and parcel of the night's work.

So it'll be business as usual but around the edges he'll be having his scene with Laura – they'll be bouncing off the four walls of this place, urgent negotiations will be under way, both of them will be suffering loss and suchlike difficulties.

He looks around, here where he's worked and played-away-from-home for a while now. He supposes it's a fit enough place to hold a bust-up in, after all. There's been enough broken love affairs in this saloon not to mention gambling arguments and marriages going down the tube and staff members on the blink and physical fights, most of them started with a pint and a cigarette to hand if not finished that way exactly, but instead with people sprawled on the carpet or thrown out by their ears usually. The worst he ever saw was between the wee scrap-iron merchant fellow, Albert, a wiry Englishman who fought the good fight in the war, and the young German who took to drinking in Albert's own pub, this very Dreghorn Castle, accompanied by his teenage daughter some fifty years later

– but perhaps Albert didn't hear about the Armistice because he'd cross behind the pair of them and say, Tart, in a loud voice, week in, week out, to excite the German, in which he was successful, the muttering growing to shouting matches between them still with this Tart word every now and again thrown in by Albert to keep the soup on the boil until eventually the younger man leapt up one night with the smallest penknife anyone had ever seen held open in front of him, the blade only an inch long but even so probably still enough to stick Albert to the wall he was that thin, whereupon Albert let fly with two or three pool balls, hurling them from clear across the other side of the bar, missing the German but hitting other people, and as if by magic, with the odd shouted, Hey! and some growling the two contenders were manoeuvred outside by a general agreement among the Irish contingent for them to finish out there, the Dreghorn Castle's regulars moving then from window to window to see the progress of the fight and Ray only stepping in – the hand of God, if you like – when the young German had poor old Albert by the throat and was pressing the life out of him in the gutter. Albert kept coming to the Dreghorn Castle but the German wasn't seen again; you could ask yourself who won the contest, all in all.

So the pub as an institution can be seen surely as like the boxing ring of life; Larry imagines ropes instead of walls and the pictures of the participants in the more renowned battles pinned to the walls, moody black and white shots; while the very smell in here is a constant reminder of the smoke and the drink that's gone into the carpet and the slowly staining ceiling and the curtains strung on poles hanging halfway up the windows – Larry imagines it to be penetrating the plasterwork, you'd need to take a Kango and strip the place back to the brickwork to eradicate all vestiges of the jollity and drunkenness and noise and anger and human fight that's gone on in here over the years. No doubt he, Larry, has made his own mark before tonight; he was smoking forty a day until a year ago and he's certain to have slopped altogether a few pints of Guinness on to the floor. He imagines his contributions rubbing shoulders with others', all jostling for space and soaking into the fabric of the place.

Thinking about fighting and making up and happiness or the lack of it, Larry asks the very just and merciful God who obviously rules over this public house, why couldn't Laura respond to the Landlord, instead of the three of them having this triangle business with Ray watching Laura as though she's a meal with chips and extra sauce which's going to be taken away from him and Laura at the second point of the triangle involved with himself, Larry Azure, standing a touch shambolic but nonetheless reasonably talented on the guitar and so on and with the gift of the geg, at the third point? What turns her off Ray – the lick of hair on his collar, the trampled heels of his shoes or his beer belly being heavier than Larry's? Maybe she doesn't read him ... but she must know that when Ray keeps her glass fresh and fires up her cigarettes it's not something he does for anybody else. Mary, Mother of God, why can't some fairness come into the scheme of things, he wonders, and Laura turn about face and go for the Landlord who really needs her and who could take some joy out of the situation even if it would have to be a secret affair, with the Landlord's wife Brenda upstairs there drinking herself into a more disaffected but nonetheless devouring woman. In Larry's opinion, there'd be a justice in the tempting of Ray whatever came of it – not to mention, it'd save him some trouble this evening. Instead, Laura fixed on him, who has such a wife at home making life happy, truly so, and with Laura's full-on sexiness right close by now, he can feel the sway of danger, the dread of a bad result on his decision to break with her, which will mean his walking out of here with his tail between his legs.

At the thought of failure, Larry feels lifted by anger – if he does may he be damned for ever, *the Lord prepareth such a one for the sword* and so he'd be cast into hell on earth; all that'll be left for him is to complain and entertain vicious thoughts and imagine rubberwear.

He has an itching in his palms.

Come on, Laura, where are you? he mutters under his breath while casting his eye around; they're without a customer yet and it's all quiet except for the Landlord's fiddling with the till and the noises from outside – the sewing-machine-like moped engine of the Chinese delivery boy and the smack of his rear tyre on the road as he drives off the kerb and the rattle of the top-box with the Chinese takeaway leaking sweet-n-sour inside it no doubt, and now an ambulance siren in the distance, a common enough sound as there's a regular supply of the ill and the wounded to the hospital up the road.

Then, there's the usual plumb depth yawning in the empty bar like an animal's mouth opening because he and the Landlord can hear Laura approaching. The two men listen to the scrape of feet against the cellar steps, then comes the pause that means she's tussling with the catch which is set too high up the door on the downhill side and next the creak of the hinges, slightly higher pitched on the door's return journey because of the fire-regulation spring mechanism pushing it; afterwards there's silence more or less as she must be walking along the carpet which leads to the very spot which both Larry and the Landlord are watching now – the mirrored doorway leading out to the back area.

It's as though a gunman were going to walk into the saloon, no less.

Ray's straightened his shoulders.

Larry's tucking his shirt in and hauling on the back of his trousers.

They're both having to steady themselves because Laura's entrances are an event however hard she tries to downplay them, but this one, from the dark slot leading out to the corridor and stairwell and the general area where the coats are kept, is bizarre suddenly because all Larry sees, instead of a fit young woman whom he's secretly and illegally fucked to death on these very premises for a year or more, is this pink Saint Valentine's heart emerging, Laura's hand being clipped to the leading edge; she is almost obscured by the polystyrene decoration, this giant symbol; Christ, what a cruelty when it's the one part of him that's never engaged with her, his heart-n-soul, and here she is waving the truth like it's a big flagged-up warning to him, saying look she has got one after all, a heart, and he's not to trifle with it or else, look how big a thing it is.

As the heart emerges, as it were, with its human legs, he can see her other hand holding the back end while underneath her leather boots move back and forth comically.

Ray the Landlord sings, Love is in the air . . . He gives a wink and claps his hand to his chest.

Laura answers cynically, Oh yeah. Love. That's what it's all about.

Larry's glad, hearing her say that – isn't it to his advantage that she's a bit off about the whole love thing; won't it make it easier to throw a spanner in the works?

Now she's manoeuvring out of the hatchway and Larry can see her from top to bottom, briefly. Her face, Larry tells himself, this time for God's sake remember to look at her face instead of the legs or whatever, because sometimes he wouldn't know what colour her eyes are, even, if he was invited on to the TV chat show that challenges married people on that type of thing.

Look at her, the glory of it, she has just the right ounce or two of flesh under the skin, which gives her that perfect soft body you see in the magazines, the blonde hair now, whereas it was dark before, parted in the middle hanging in a cowl or bell shape from the wide headbands she's taken to wearing all the time like girls in the '60s used to, her lips straight but capable of moving, he knows, from the usual deadpan position to a frown more usually but sometimes a smile, on the few occasions she does alter her expression.

But she's not giving him any sign of recognition, which is what he expects, because he's just put out and winked at her in the moment before she turns again to aim for where the decoration is put up every year, on the far wall behind the entertainers' podium.

At the same time he lifts his hand to his forehead in a futile attempt to stop himself from doing the winking or at least to hide it from her; he shouldn't do that when he's going to blast her out of the water, shortly. Here he is already trying to avoid trouble when he should be walking towards it.

He thinks, Christ, even she was a baby once and came out of the womb, what a thought.

With that straight face she's wearing and not a glimmer of satisfaction at seeing him even, it occurs to him, maybe she's going to dump on him first.

The idea shocks him something fearful. For Chrissakes, if that's the case he should get a move on so as to feel it's his doing, otherwise it won't be anything like the experience it should be, nor will it carry the same message in his heart.

While Larry's panicking, Ray can now ogle her rear view while pretending not to, the rounded bum promising such good times that the sight of it short-circuits his nervous system.

If Ray is trying to imagine what's under those leggings – Larry knows. At the same time as being soft, her body is workmanlike, solidly built, like it's been places; she has a strong walk and looks useful, not prissy. She's wearing a waisted top, glittery, pinched by a belt or cummerbund affair. This blouse is saved for the more special of the Dreghorn Castle's celebrations and here's Larry, about to turn on the cold water tap all right, choosing a different path in the wood.

Laura leans down to rest the heart against the wall and with that small dip of her back flaring her hips suddenly – the spine kept straight meanwhile, as women can – Larry is reminded of the porno photies where the girls lean forward in a similar way except they're looking over their shoulders, always with dreamy smiles and wearing all the kit while they get done in various ways, by one man or a gang of men or men and women all joining in together in a more whole-hearted party-style event, lots of hips bouncing back and forth and hands pillaging breasts or in extreme close-up loads of cocks plugging away, all so that ordinary folk can imagine they're the ones walking in on a bit of a scene having been given the wrong hotel key or stumbling on a young lady caught up in wire on a country ramble or imprisoning a woman executive in an empty office with several of their friends, pinning her down only to find she offers more than they dreamt of or finding the girl with the wet T-shirt on the beach who doesn't want to know their names and shows her breasts before telling them she only enjoys it sideways with a couple of nuns watching.

Christ, isn't sex a witty trade, thinks Larry. As it is, you have to stop yourself from wondering how much everyone got paid and what they said when they first met before the cameras were switched on, and that's a tasty thought, that people can get together as a result of no more than a bunch of fivers changing hands, then these things can happen, the gratification that crude and unhappy and mechanical, when the coming is just like a swear word – *fuck* – that escapes with no morality value or any other thought attached to it other than let's get this out of the way and move on to the next thing and meanwhile get paid.

As he and the Landlord watch, Laura is taking hold of a chair and she now positions it for her convenience against the skirting. Stepping on to it and finding her balance, she lifts the heart and holds it against the wall above her. Christ, what a sight, her stretching upwards like that.

What would it have been, their own porno film, starring himself and Laura? It's been shot only on the premises of the Dreghorn Castle, in the stockroom and in the staff toilet and so on and taken on the hoof without any planning that's for sure, so it's been hurried to say the least, there's no prizes due them for the romantic and slow approach; when they've only had two minutes it's been hotter and fiercer than when they've been allowed five, which he supposes if it says anything, means he wants to escape from it soonest.

He accuses himself, you've been like a dog with a bone, Larry; now, are you going to let go of it? Yes, he replies, and quick about it before she does the business on you –

but he can't talk to her yet, they have to be alone or in
such a crowd and noise as to be able to feel private, don't
they?

Trying to forge ahead like this Larry sees it's not going
to be as easy as he thought to give her the push, now he's
in here, because to do that is not only to kick her in the
teeth but also he'll be demoting himself as it were, turning
his back on the general sense of wonder and awe that
people-in-the-know have, jealous that he, Larry Azure, is
enjoying the prize barmaid here, so it's not just a question
of putting up a hand and saying, Thanks but no thanks,
Laura, he'll have to step down from others' estimation and
join the throng, an ordinary mortal, which will be a hard
knock.

Plus, you might have to do extra homework if you want
to catch up on living cleanly, he tells himself, because you'll
be a touch rusty.

Laura is letting the polystyrene heart slide downwards
slowly, then lifting it again – faster on the upward stroke –
in her attempt to snag the wire at the back on the nail and
so hang it on the wall, but she's failing so far. This up-
and-down movement of hers, continuing with such an even
rhythm, together with the occasional self-absorbed murmur
and grunting from her as she carries on, is enough to
have Larry suddenly think it's like it's a fucking great big
imaginary cock she's holding, but not his, tonight, he
swears, the game's up.

Glancing at the Landlord, he sees the latter's jaw's dropped open, he's stopped dead on his way to changing the

mini toilet roll in the cash till and is watching her, just standing there like a big kid in his electric-blue nylon tracksuit bottoms and his Garfield T-shirt ruffled by the breeze from the portable fan standing on the bar, even in winter.

Laura is standing on the chair with her legs a touch apart and her arms crucified.

Bloody hell, she's exclaiming with some urgency and a note of request in her voice.

What? asks Larry.

I can't keep this up, my arms are going, she warns.

These words click with a memory of Larry's; because it's what she said to him once, wasn't it, I can't keep this up, while they were larking about on the stairs leading down to the cellar, she standing a step or two below him, smacked by the weirdness of not having a scrap of privacy and the wretched winebox was under her other arm; so the blood had left his cock like a plug had been pulled from the bottom of it because he was one or two over the limit as well.

Then Laura adds, still pressed against the wall there and moving the decoration up and down and talking to it, Come on, hurry up.

This is too much of a coincidence – because again Larry's memory is snagged: he and Laura were scrabbling about on the stockroom floor unable to get it together because her hair was all in her face and his trouser zip was stuck fast making the whole effort ridiculous when she said just those words, didn't she? Is she repeating these phrases that are known to them both in order to send a message to him – instead of smiling and so on she's giving away moments they've shared during fun times?

Larry Azure is puzzled; he watches her more closely.

He and the Landlord can both see the inch of bare flesh at her waist, with the blouse and her cummerbund lifting because of the extra effort she's putting into her work.

Then Laura's caught the nail with the string and she's on and off the chair several times like in an aerobics class, to make sure it's straight, her stomach still showing when she turns round, her navel a neat button there in the roundness of her stomach like a single eye staring at them with almost the deadpan expression she has herself.

The Landlord stands there, twiddling the roll of paper while Laura takes a last look at her handiwork. Then she steps down from the podium and rubs the dust from the tips of her fingers.

She asks, Is that OK?

The business, calls Ray.

Sure enough, the heart is straight and centred; and she herself will be up there with Ray doing the raffle at some point.

The Landlord's up to something different now behind the bar; Larry can see his hands working away. It's almost suspicious.

No, don't worry, I'll get the raffle bucket, insists Laura, her ironic tone telling them not to move a muscle and let her do all the work – and it wasn't said in a lighthearted way at all – while she's walking back the way she came.

Larry wonders who's jerked her chain.

As she goes she's tugging her top down and fidgeting with the belt, while suddenly Ray's mixed her a drink already, with magic speed considering he'll have chopped an orange and got the ice out of the bucket, and he's lifting it in the air like he's toasting her.

He calls matter-of-factly, Here y'are, Miss Brighton Beach Belle.

He's referring to a beauty title she won while on holiday, she was telling them once.

She doesn't veer towards the drink. Thanks, she replies, while leaving it in his hand; she's still on her way.

So as not to lose face Ray slides it down the bar a ways and says, Cheers, without a trace of disappointment.

Then she's gone again.

In the silence that follows, Larry looks around. It feels like a lot ought to have happened but everything's the same: the beermats and ashtrays are still in place, the curtains are drawn and the blackboard for the darts score and the pool rota is wiped clean.

The tension drains from Larry's shoulders.

The Landlord, he notices, has had to light up a Marlboro.

Following his lead, Larry sits at a table in the middle of the lounge, takes out a Silk Cut and fires it up using his treasured icon, the petrol lighter he got for his birthday five years ago.

Then they're both motionless except for the smoking, looking at the empty spot where it all happened.

They need a rest after the excitement.

Five minutes later, with his cigarette sucked down to the stub and a moment or two's rest on top of that, Larry takes his courage in both hands. This is it. With Laura not coming back as quick as she should, it's the usual message for him to come and meet her downstairs, where they can be alone.

He heads for the back. He stops and starts again, stops, fiddles with a corner of the picture of the 1994 Ireland football squad pinned to the door, then spurs himself into going on.

Christ, that he can be like a teenager still, with his hands this heavy and leaden and a sickness in the middle of him at having to confront her – who would have thought it from a middle-aged DJ-singer-entertainer with a first-class degree in philosophy from the Belfast polytechnic who's after all let a few mistresses run through his fingers by now.

So he's on the way to the cellar, calling to Ray to give his alibi, I'll line up the kegs on the Directors and the 6X.

Sure now? asks Ray.

Larry jokes, Save you wearing out your broken-backed slippers there, Ray.

The Landlord calls, Thanks a million, they've to last me all next year as you know.

So Larry is pushing through the door when he jumps with fright, seeing this strange figure in the corridor.

In that instant he's thinking – the notion bouncing sideways every other thought of Laura and the scene he's to have with her – it's a raid just like the Landlord suffered before, with the stranger here carrying a knife probably and should he run or not, when he sees it's a girl, and he calms down – only a notch though because in any case there's a member of the public where by rights one shouldn't be and who knows what a drug-crazed teenager could do to him; he's read the reports of the cow-tranquilliser drug the kids enjoy taking in LA which gives old ladies even the strength of ten men – this girl could probably throw him through the wall and plough on with robbing every poor guy in the place.

All this wasn't a leisurely queue of thoughts, it was more an instant's reading of the dangerous situation confronting him.

He stares; the woman stares back. She has ratty hair in short tufts like the bums and street kids and dope-heads whom the Landlord's always shaking his fists at in this neck of the woods, which has meant the pub's windows have had to be replaced with Perspex instead of glass to stop the bricks coming through.

Larry thinks, she'll be after the money in the coat pockets hanging in the corridor or maybe she was hoping to get as far as the stores or the cellar and run off with some alcohol prizes for herself and her friends to share out or sell on.

A fraction of a second later he's aware that by coincidence or as part of the scam, the stranger is wearing Laura's clothes: the same top and leggings. She has a familiar figure ... astonished, Larry feels his mouth close all by itself and say the word, Laura, because it's her all right and that means there's an emergency here – where's her hair gone? Why isn't she saying anything and what's wrong with her?

In the dimness of the corridor he watches as Laura stoops and picks something up from the floor. Standing and making one deft movement – a wipe over her head from front to back – she's replaced the wig.

Larry is three paces closer now as she's tugging the hairband into place. He repeats, Laura.

Now he understands what he was looking at: she's having to wear a wig for some reason; it's attached to the hairband so no one will see the join at her forehead and he's not noticed in the past few months she's taken to wearing it all the time, he thought it was just dyed a different colour and he made a joke or two which had flown past her, which is her way of dealing with his teasing her in any case, so he didn't notice any extra touchiness on her part about it.

He watches while she packs away a compact mirror and replaces it in the pocket of her coat.

He swears, Christ.

He asks, How come, you know, with the hair, there?

She looks at him and he sees she's smudged her eyes;

that was what the mirror was for, to check her make-up as well. She generally thickens her eyebrows and heats up her mouth with some extra colour, anyway, but this is a whole-sale repair job.

You've been crying then, because of your hair? he asks.

Laura wants to shout at him but knows if she does, Ray will hear them so she's leaning back into the coats now and saying very quietly, You're going to leave me, Larry, you're fucking going to leave me.

Astonished, Larry asks himself how she knew, is this the famous feminine intuition at work here? He rocks back and forth on his feet. Should he say yes, she guessed right – or more urgently shouldn't he find out what's up with the hair-loss situation; he's afraid of suddenly having a reputation as the guy, did you hear about him, who had the mistress who had the brain tumour and only a week or two left to live, but he dumped her anyway?

What he wants more than anything is to avoid making more trouble than he has to. He asks in a friendly fashion, What's up, Laura, with the wig and so on, does it mean you're ill?

Stress, she answers, as though directing the reply to the ceiling light fitting right there above her which is casting this gloomy shadow, more than any light. Then she's turn-ing on him and doing this prediction thing again, loudly, You might not know it right now but you and I aren't going to be together any more, not that we ever fucking were.

Listen, Laura, he begins, but she's straightaway inter-

rupting, quietly, but menacing him, You're going to leave
me, yes or no, Larry.

She's levered herself away from the coats and is coming
close enough for him to see where the tears were wiped
on to her face and still sit in the rim of her eyes, next to
breaking out again, and she's murmuring, Just give me a
yes or no, not the usual bollocks, just one fucking simple
word.

He begins, What in hell's brought this on? but she's
down his throat again, insisting, One word! and stamping
her foot, but the hurt's there, as well as the anger.

Go on, Larry, he tells himself, say it, it's clearly a gift
from God, that she should want to jump from the cliff he
was anyway going to push her over and he should remind
himself she's a mistress not a wife, that they were both
playing the same game, the illicit affair, and there wasn't
any romantic scenery behind either of them if truth be
known.

She repeats, You're going to leave me, Larry, yes or no,
say it?

After some moments of dumb staring and shuffling from
foot to foot, Larry says, Well, yes.

He feels it's the wrong thing even to blink then as she's
looking at him so hard – to test his hold on the answer
he's given, it must be.

She repeats, Yes . . . just like that?

He points out, You asked for it just like that, you did, so.

Then she's come up to him and delicately put one arm
around his neck and he can feel her arrival against him.

He holds off a touch, so she leans into him some more. She's saying, One more time.

Larry guesses it's all right to give her a goodbye kiss and is closing on her mouth when he feels the jab of her knuckles in his ribs, hard.

She swears, Fuck off.

Then she's on her way back to the bar and Larry's left holding his side where she hit him.

With the door open and looking back at him she's calling over her shoulder in her best polite voice for Ray's benefit, D'you think you could get the raffle bucket, Larry?

And then a second later she adds, Thanks.

Larry's left with silence, just the coats hanging here and the air still charged with what happened.

Clutching his side he's saying to himself, Never mind the pain, Larry – is that it? Done with in a trice like that?

In some disbelief he continues the mission to the cellar, the twinge in his ribs subsiding quickly.

There must be more – what's happened to the almighty row they're to have?

As he negotiates the steps he's that sure she'll be following him with a blunt instrument, so he turns around – but there's no one there.

Continuing downwards, he can still feel her eyes on his back. Earlier he was thinking she's a ghost put there to tempt him, but right now he's expecting something a little more concrete – some screaming and tears, the least of it.

Shaking his head, he remembers – And she's lost her hair somehow?

He takes a breath or two and weighs up the situation.

He said yes, he's leaving her, clear as anything.

She heard him, sure she did.

So it's over, isn't it?

Then perhaps he should simply give himself a pat on the back – after all, he's done what he had to and ended it.

Christ, he'd built it up too much, hadn't he – it was more a problem in his mind than in real life, the confrontation with her. Wasn't it easy as pie in effect? He ducked in and delivered the knock-out blow and that was that. Success. One word he did it with – Yes. Jut a simple word of truth from the great Larry Azure there – and not many minutes after he'd walked into the pub this evening swearing he'd do just that.

There was nothing to be afraid of. He did more than OK.

Full steam ahead, Larry.

So he's lining up the kegs on the 6X and the Directors and while he's about it he can fetch out the raffle bucket himself, he's feeling that up for business and jollity now.

Great, A1, that's it, he's muttering while stumbling among the bits of timber and the general debris cluttering the rear wall of the cellar. And it's because he had the wherewithal to stand against Laura and tell her the one big word, yes, that he can write off the whole Laura thing, it was youthful antics surely – and not only that, but now he can straightaway move on and claim the reward: himself an upright man deserving his wife, *what therefore God hath joined together, let not man put asunder*, and this, Larry, is the promise waiting for you, he tells himself, now you're walking down the chosen path with already the sunshine playing at your feet and the outlook fair for the start of your family.

7.30 p.m.

It's a whisker past seven-thirty now and that being the time when the plug's well and truly pulled on the last working day of the week and the flow of people starts, their share of the beleaguered city who've fought their way in here for mass escapism and entertainment, there'll be more and more drinkers and members of Larry's public coming in, plus those who choose by accident to step into this pub on the windswept corner and stay long enough to surprise themselves hopefully and to warm their cockles at the sight of Laura's body and the way it moves and maybe catch the live entertainment: two half-hour-long sets with a raffle in between – Tonight, Larry Azure! the singer will be announced as, the Landlord more likely than not collaring the microphone again to say in his London-Irish voice, And if that's his real name, I'm bleedin' Gloria Estefan, or suchlike.

But for now Ray the Landlord aims the remote at the TV set clamped high on the wall and at the same time gives his short, piercing whistle which has the drinkers clamping their hands over their ears – he likes people to think it's the whistle and not the on-button which starts the telly rampaging through its material there in the corner.

The three of them working the bar might be counted as workmates but the truth is they're in their own heads and only part of them is open for public inspection; the big curly-haired singer with his sharply sloping, rounded shoulders and the even more overweight one treading heavily through the heels of his shoes and the girl with the cleavage who keeps still all the time as though hoping no one will notice she's there and make a move on her are more or less an everyday sight, but nothing's known beyond their names and curiously enough the intimate thing of what clothes they possess, since working here every night brings each garment in turn out of their wardrobes, eventually.

Laura is leaning, cupping her cigarette, squinting into the smoke. Then she stands up straight to fold a white apron to quarter-length, before tying the swath around her hips, which only adds to her attraction.

Not even suspecting Laura's hair isn't her own but a wig hanging from the hairband, far less knowing his bar staff have been having an affair on the premises under his nose for a year, the Landlord passes behind her exclaiming, Let's sell beer, and he's patting Larry as well on the back, on his way to the mirror to comb his hair, so he'll be presentable shortly.

Larry shifts his weight from one foot to the other so it looks like he's ready for business and maybe he is but also he's daydreaming, perhaps about having enough money soon to leave the barwork for good and count it as done with, he'll be a pro DJ and entertainer.

They're all present and correct; and Ray the Landlord – with his side parting straight as an arrow now – is leaning his knuckles on the bar and looking down to where Larry is also sprawled but in an opposite fashion, backwards, with his fingers halfway in his pockets. The *Coronation Street* theme music is playing and Ray is nodding his head and gives a smile because here they are in a real pub when the nation's watching the soap-opera pub, the Rovers Return, so they're all walking the same side of life at this moment, Ray and his pub and his customers as well as the characters in *Coronation Street* and the millions watching them.

Ray likes this sense of being team-leader, it suits him, the same way he can take the warm-up exercises for the local football league team and keep the darts outing on the road to arrive at the right place in good time.

Larry gets the message, this is Ray's goodwill coming at him and he lifts his thumb in a return gesture.

Tending her smaller side of the L-shaped bar Laura misses the celebratory mood, which is no surprise after all; how would the signal get through when she's so blanked off from the others? She leans forward and by a lucky accident this means her rear, neatly wrapped in its white flag, gives a wave from one side to the other as she shifts her weight. Some signal this is; all the men who can are watching.

If Ray's wife Brenda happened to be staring into her gin and tonic upstairs at the moment and could see through the bottom of her glass and through the floorboards to the scene below she'd perceive her old habitat, the Dreghorn

Castle bar, filling up now, sure enough, people clustered in
the same fashion, it's always been the same way: a crowding
around the girl barmaid, she being hired as that template
which fits men just right, the young males driven beside
themselves which is unfair on any other women in the
place, the older men admiring ruefully from a distance and
judging youth to be wasted on the young and imagining
what they could do that'd be so much better, with all their
experience and wisdom; if they were only allowed to get
hold of her they'd frighten the teeth from her gums all
right, wouldn't they, with all the tricks they know, and yet
some young sod who doesn't know his arse from his elbow
would be all that'd be getting a look-in.

Central among these older and more experienced men
and standing six foot two in his boots as though a pole to
which the rest of them are attached is Mike the Bike;
having staked his territory here he won't be moved while
around him are gathered Laura's younger and more avid
lookers-on.

Laura herself plays the crowd pressing around her now
with this technique she's refined out of long practice – after
all she had to start slapping boys down aged twelve at
school discos so it's second nature for her not to be caught
in anyone's gaze. She mostly looks at the drinks she's lining
up on the bar or at the notes handed to her and the change
she gives back, even when she's prompted into talking. If a
smile is called for she'll take care to aim it at the rack of
glasses above her head or at the ice bucket as she nudges
it to whomever, straightening her mouth to its normal

deadpan line, to prevent anyone thinking they might have a chance with it, because that's what her mouth is after all, a first port of call in any triumph over her. These men buzzing around her like flies – it's a waste of time and stops any humour in its tracks and turns every smile and spoken word into a full-on sexual assault. She could do without it.

The outskirts of the room are less densely populated; there are small groups around the tables and the first few names are chalked up for the pool table and the darts board, the players revolving slowly, the men it seems without much concern for the women, but the opposite is the case maybe; even a darts match is a long-winded game deciding who's going to score as it were, who's going to take which woman home and vice versa. The elderly blind man, Tom, has his usual corner from where he'll probably launch his own oddball sex attack later on, which the whole bar will have to put up with, but for now he greets passers-by; he is especially happy to talk to any dogs that come his way because they'll give him longer and more considered attention than well-meaning neighbours and if they keep pawing him he'll carry on until closing time, smiling, bent over this or that collie or mongrel. Niall's dog, Lucky, doesn't leave her spot however on Niall's coat at his feet; although she makes eyes at the other dogs like she's going to allow them to love her to death, she'll walk straight past them a moment later or simply not bother to stand up if they come over to sniff her out.

Now Ray is on his way to the till, where he bangs the keypad to open it and rummage for change for the jukebox.

This first song he puts on courtesy of the Dreghorn Castle is always the same: Elkie Brooks sings 'Beautiful'. There are cries and moans of objection from the *Coronation Street* fans and a loud voice calls, No no, Raymond.

Larry feels the lift of the music and respects it, how it fuels the Castle, suddenly gearing it differently, there's that vitality which before was absent and ordinary objects are transformed into more romantic versions of themselves; the keys there hanging from Niall's belt-loop might open the gates to his soul now, you could say, or some such notion; Mike the Bike's leather jerkin is his armour, Tom's stick is a friend keeping him on the straight and narrow. When Larry's in the studio this Sunday with the pop confection Whigfield as his guest star he'll introduce her by telling his listeners about his theory that music equals glamour, play a good song and it has the same effect as a beautiful woman walking into the room and joining your table, it gladdens all of us and we feel twice the people we were before, so if there's no lovely lady for you, stay close to the song, to Elkie Brooks here with us tonight and it's the same, she'll make you feel more than usually fine as an individual and as one among others in society, sharing the sound with Niall and Tom and the Bike here, fine people. Elkie, tell us how you do it, so many of us want to and yet so few know the trick of it.

So, with the curtains drawn and the windows shut and all the lights burning and the games begun and the music started up on this Saint Valentine's night, Friday the fourteenth, the 'public house' as it's rightly called fronts the inhumanity of the windswept corner here with the drugs dealers lounging importantly in the darkness only yards away and the youths' motors squealing past and the rain standing black in puddles, perhaps because of the dirt it's pulled out of the sky. The music, the talk, the game-play, the blood heat of the place, is contained within foam-insulated double-skinned brick walls and a painted sign warns the untouchable, the unforgiven and the unhappy that this is the Dreghorn Castle, beware, it's for good cheer only.

No no, keep hold of it, cries Larry, it's slippery as hell.

The Landlord leans his bulky frame against the one-armed bandit. Larry is to climb via a table set next to it and from there on to the top.

Will the thing hold together? asks Larry, before he sets off.

I dare say, replies the Landlord.

If I fall, I'll be suing you for a million.

I shall open the till, Larry, and empty my pockets if you bruise so much as a buttock.

Thank you for that.

So Larry climbs on to the wee table set adjacent to the fruit machine with its fantasy menu of electronic riffs and lighted panels still going, fooling Niall, it is, at the moment, into thinking he's closer to winning – and when he's made the climb on to the machine itself, the television is just near enough to hand for him to reach the aerial cable. He begins to wiggle it, and the mute picture jumps and flickers.

This cable, thinks Larry as he's stretched to breaking point, it's a tunnel that goes into the same general traffic as everything else, let no one forget the airwaves are working all around them, in every frequency, this TV receiver here bolted to the wall can catch the UHF and the VHF and the MW and the LW. Wagging away at the faulty aerial cable with the Landlord shouting advice from below, Larry wonders what the waves, the actual things themselves, look like and seeing the static lines on this faulty TV set he judges if they could be seen they'd appear like that surely, the air scored through from side to side or perhaps slantwise like rain or alternatively it would be more random, like looking through scratched glass in a flickering light. Plus – and here's a thought – did the airwaves exist before radio and TV, so the stations just hitched a ride on what was already buzzing around, or is the atmosphere filling up with more and more as they come on air, the glass becoming more scratched?

You done? calls Ray.

It needs perhaps a nail because it likes to sit, like so, Larry demonstrates, lifting the cable, which, because the jack at the back of the set is loose, gives them a better picture. D'you see?

What about just loop it over the top of the set there – is there enough slack?

But when Larry's succeeded in doing this, he looks down

from his perch on top of the one-armed bandit to find they've taken the table away.

Hey, he begins, my table back, you bozos.

There's no one wants you down here, jokes Ray who's some distance away now, not holding on to the gaming machine at all. There's a revolution against that show of yours, he adds.

That's funny, my audience is going up, Ray.

Ray replies, People are saying you're to be taught a lesson so here y'are. Talk your way out of that one.

Larry looks down at the smattering of people beneath him. They're enjoying the joke, he can spot a smile or two and they're waiting to see what he'll do. Niall puts another coin into the slot and asks, Can you hop up and down a bit and maybe it'll help the money come out?

Larry catches Laura's eye behind the bar while she's slapping the wine cooler to try and stop it from making its buzzing noise and it strikes him, he should ask her for help, as a start, anyway, to re-opening communications; he's consumed with a need for her forgiveness – *forgive men their trespasses*, he should remind her. He wants to buy her a drink. He calls out, Laura, bring the wee table here, will you? which is a mistake because now she ignores him and so everyone's reading this, thinking what's up between those two, so he's scundered, a touch, and has to hop down by himself, the floor jarring him from his heels up, the effect made worse from feeling downcast about the Laura situation.

But then as he dusts himself down and stamps his feet

to make the shoes sit straight after the drop, he tells himself to leave well alone, ignore her, he shouldn't even be
looking sideways to where he'd be on the other path if
he'd taken it, the one with Laura and her like on it, because
at this early stage it's still close enough for him to step over
and regain it with no more than a moment's discomfort, in
terms of a doubt or two and the regret of a resolution
broken. Until he's deep enough into the new Larry Azure,
human being, he tells himself, don't worry about the guilt,
keep your head down, Larry, and you'll walk out of here
on two legs with a conscience cleared and ready to go –
Christ, it sounds like a luxury, truly – so this is maybe the
meat and drink of the mighty battle tonight: the avoiding
of Laura. Don't touch, don't anything, defend and hang on
to the early lead you've won for yourself, Larry. The easy
part's done with, now it's the tough, long-drawn-out
defence.

He remembers when he was playing Sunday football his
team had this habit, if they netted the first goal, to be that
excited they nigh on forgot to play at all in the ensuing
minutes so the other side would come haring back and
score twice before they knew it.

So, taking a parallel argument with this Laura situation
as he's come to think of it, the trick will be to adopt an
all-out defensive position and crowd the goalmouth.

He remembers as well, it was a near thing anyway –
wasn't it almost that she gave him the push and not the
other way round, he was ducking in there for a last kiss of
all things – which is like an alcoholic saying just one more

before I give it up completely, so help me God – when she jabbed him in the ribs. The battle wasn't won so convincingly as he thought maybe so yes it should be a superhuman effort now to defy temptation, not to succumb to remorse, to avoid Laura tonight.

Should he tuck himself away and telephone his wife, just to turn himself away from Laura, a touch?

He answers himself no.

Christ, Larry swears as he registers the growing volume of voices and the movement of people coming in and shouting orders, what's happening here is that everyone's chasing like mad for sex, he can feel it in the air, all the erections starting up, the fannies unfurling like in the speeded-up films on the Open University showing how flowers work, it's the start of that anyway, fuelled by the alcohol, that's what's going on; everyone's preparing to get fucked and all the men's cocks are pointing at Laura at least part of the time, before swinging round to targets they might actually have more of a chance with, whereas this distant dream all the men have, of sampling Laura's favours, he himself has just given up; would anyone believe that if they knew?

But think, Larry – how not to have a relapse, here?

Certainly he's not got any new ideas, he'll be the first to admit, only the same ones he's been through a time or two before but he should trawl through his experience of closing down on the women to see what might help.

Without realising, he's taken a seat at a table by himself and then, instead of his hands folded in his lap it's his microphone and Larry'd be pleased if it's more than once a week, his late-night show, with millions listening instead of the current few thousands. He'll say, Calm down and stop fighting among yourselves, there's someone for every-body, ladies and gentlemen; look, a man with sloping shoulders and curly black hair such as myself, with a certain gift for the guitar, has found a wife to love him, and that's a man without riches and with the jeans hanging low enough around his arse to make him look like a Murphy's cable contractor and road digger, although of course the differ-ence is, my particular buttocks are deceptively small, charming like a boy's, so all of you out there listen to me now, it's your job to listen and mine to talk to you: Gentle-men, share the ladies out; if you're winning more than your share, let go and allow the others their chance of happiness. Ladies, if you're well and truly surrounded by the gentle-men and so a subject of envy, think of your sisters who are currently doing without and may their prayers be answered and they win someone of their own to keep and to love them. This passing notion of mine, explains Larry, inspired the next song which I hope will strike you as worth the terrible long time I spent concocting it . . .

The Landlord's calling him to get over here and do some useful fucking work, Larry, for a change; Ray's always been a touch aggrieved that Larry's adding-up is faultless, how-ever long a string of drinks anyone orders Larry never gets it wrong on account of his memory, he can hold the decimal point in the right place and keep the figures clicking up accurate as a computer whereas the Landlord, the guv'nor after all, falters every time he crosses over the pennies and the pounds, even after this long, so he has a pencil and paper – and on top of that now Larry's landed the Talk Radio job, which Ray has refused to listen to.

With Ray's shout, Larry's head lifts and he's surprised to find himself still sitting at one of the tables which are like mini-oases for the thirsty currently struggling to get themselves here – as though he wasn't working at all. He's been that in-his-own-head to dream along like he's driving on the motorway, when you come off automatic mode truly fucking head-shakingly amazed not to have had a smash and wondering where on earth you are. Sure enough though, the Dreghorn Castle is still here; the lights are on and the tables are half busy now, meanwhile the Landlord can be heard crackling away refilling the crisps boxes under the bar with the various flavours.

If Ray asks what's he been up to, he'll say he's doing some of that market research into what it's like this side of the business. The stool is a touch hard, he'll report. The table here is like plastic to the touch, what with the million or so coats of varnish on it. And all these people were babies once – Larry keeps on finding that overall philosophy popping up in his head like when he was looking at the gingery fellow in the Chinese and the same goes for every other soul walking or talking in the entire world, for the sake of Christ isn't that a notion and a half all right. Ray the Landlord there who's up and walking and talking – a mother and maybe a father once wiped his arse and carried him back and forth and paid out money until their pockets were inside out and their faces lined with grief and effort. Someone woke up in the night for that over-weight beer addict and darts player there who's leaning his knuckles on the bar and soothed him, believe it or not. Then Larry has the thought, maybe no one did pay any attention to Ray's wife, Brenda, when she was a baby and perhaps they put a spot of brandy in her milk to make her sleep, but still she was kept going in whatever haphaz-ard fashion, all along the line, to reach where she is now.

So isn't it a thought, Larry, that if you're sticking to this path with the starting-a-family racket only a touch further along, you're going to bring another landlord or alcoholic into the world? What's it going to be, a driver or a mechanic or a musician or what? He doesn't mind at all, the only notion he cares about is, will it find someone to love, because it's a cruelty to give it breath in its body without promising that at least, because among the pulling and pushing of life itself something has to be there to cause joy in a person's soul, doesn't it, and what else is there?

Now he's finally bumped from his reverie by the Land-lord who's standing right by him and shouting again, Hey, hey! and knocking his shoulder and bluffing him into coming back to his station behind the bar.

Larry knows not to be annoyed when Ray bullies him like this, Larry's value is solid gold here at the Dreghorn Castle, in terms of the entertainment and the drinkers shouting to have him working here for Chrissake and the clutch of young people turning up now, having heard about the gig on the radio, so can't he stay put for a wee moment? He doesn't want to go near Laura.

Defence, Larry, what's your defence?

Not drinking must be the first one: *Be sober, be vigilant; because your adversary the devil, as a roaring lion, walketh about, seeking whom he may devour.* If Larry's at all in liquor, he can find himself with a hard-on in the street just looking at an all right woman turned on to him with the full kit and make-up and perfume and the right inch or two of leg or cleavage showing. However, he warns himself – and Christ, it's a stern warning, he should take notice of it – he's working in a pub for Chrissake, is it truly possible not to drink, to be a pioneer?

As Larry makes his way through the hatch to the workmanlike side of the bar and begins to patrol his station for orders, he considers how to avoid visiting this twin-headed Bacchanal-devil type of combination, the Guinness with the brandy chaser.

Run away, Larry, is the only answer he comes up with, barge through the double doors there and keep going, live on a desert island.

What if he imagines he has a car outside and has to drive home, or that he's on antibiotics or that he's taken a dose of the anti-alcohol drug that Brenda upstairs is prescribed – would any of that be a help? Then, he might only have to think of Brenda herself and shouldn't he mark the damage done to her and say he'll not drink and from that moment always shake his head and advise himself, don't go near the stuff, Larry, point number one and this time stick to it, all your face will puff up and you'll be a dog with a redder and more broken complexion until you drop dead, near purple-coloured with it, your liver split open and hard as stone.

Larry's gaze skips from one tap to the next – Heineken, 6X, Directors – and on to the rank of spirits, dwelling more on the points which succour him: the Guinness handle standing like a slim, white skittle there, and the brandy optic. For his taste he'll have one of each standing on the table in front of him, the one running down his throat after the other.

It's no wonder, anyone's manhood would be enlivened by the sight of a pint of Guinness, knowing in advance through personal experience that it's an aphrodisiac, prowess in the sack not given of course, taken away rather, but when the drink's in your blood the lust anyway has a kick like a mule.

So, sure enough, it'll be a lot of work turning it down; when the juice is in the glass it's a friendly enough looking thing, and on top of that nowadays a pint of ale looks like a fearsome technical achievement, there's turmoil in a freshly poured stout, the billowing cloud like a weather system they've devised to impress the purchaser who's paying enough after all, the powdery and granular swirl of what is it, air? before the colours separate and the foam stands gratifyingly solid, the icing on the cake as it were, at the top of the glass.

All three of the bar staff are working now, both of the men – because their hands are busy and the cigs are parked in their mouths – squinting through cigarette smoke, facing into the corners of the bar like scolded children as they hold glasses to the various taps.

Larry knows if he's not to drink it'll mean having to turn down the many generous customers who like to buy him one. They come in here to have a good time and if they're the giving sort should he entertain the notion of refusing their friendship in that way? Put yourself in their shoes, he tells himself, and he leans his weight on to the other leg watching the Directors slide into a glass, thinking, this is the arena where the customers play it out, the game of drinking, and there are faces he knows all around and proper business going on down here, which'll build to a scrum later on – and if you can't buy a drink for the barman, who can you buy one for?

Plus, what can he substitute for the buzz a drink gives him, except singing and fame and the unqualified adoration of his listeners; but even then, such satisfactions are doubled with a drink inside you, so it's hardly a watertight answer to say he'll make do with the drug of public acclaim.

Standing round-shouldered at the bar taking money from the someone who ordered the Directors, he looks up because there's the *whump* of the double doors closing and a draught of cold air suddenly and the Dreghorn Castle welcomes back one of its regular faces, Mike the Bike, who disappeared for a while to buy a chip from over the road, it looks like.

Parking his rear for a moment on the one stool behind the bar which they all share from time to time, Larry tells himself, here's the first challenge to the not-drinking idea, because it's near certain the tall man'll offer Larry a pint and then if he so much as touches a drop he'll be after interfering with Laura again – it'll go like that.

To count it as a practice run is the best thing, so, he should turn it down, the usual gift, no thank you, Bike, I'm not drinking.

Except, isn't that to refuse Mike the Bike the pleasure of seeing the singer-entertainer-barman fuelled by his contribution, as surely as you might put a coin in the jukebox?

He shakes his head. It might be a touch unfair on other people, this point number one of his, not to drink.

So perhaps should he accept it and then pour the life-giving elixir down the sink, or leave it standing there and with a nod and a wink give it to one of the many deserving senior citizens a touch later on when the Bike's looking the other way?

As though the other man was listening to Larry's thoughts, Mike the Bike lifts his glass an inch – requesting a refill.

With such a weight of responsibility on his shoulders Larry is reluctant to jump to it, nevertheless he dismounts from his stool, telling himself we all have to do things we don't want to. What's odd is, it's like he's about to cheat the man.

With the standing up just then his bollocks are trapped in his jeans and squeezed, mercifully for only a moment, as if to remind him – for Christ's sake – of the sperm he's trying to hold on to for dear life.

Mike the Bike is there holding the bar down as usual with his one hand resting on the polished surface and one foot on the rail and his chip in front of him. He has his first roll-up of the evening turning expertly in the fingers of his right hand, he's wearing his sleeveless leather jerkin over the top of his padded olive-green bomber jacket zipped halfway up, his jeans and boots are pulled on tight, he has his hair carefully combed in one silvery pelt from the top of his head back to the nape of his neck, newly washed – so all in all a fine-looking man but motionless, straight-standing and too frightening to talk to, for many people.

His aftershave makes the place smell like the inside of a sauna.

Bike, Larry greets him and the other man nods and lifts his roll-up in return. He will always gaze into the middle distance given the chance and Larry wonders what Mike sees there, something no doubt, but also it's probably down to shyness, if it's an avoiding of looking anywhere else where there might be people. Larry judges it to be that also which is responsible for the perfectly clean and neat aspect of this man; he cares what might be thought of him and won't risk anything.

Larry continues, It's a fine night for a pint of ale and some tobacco.

As soon as the words are out of his mouth, he realises it sounded like he was prompting an offer of exactly that for himself, a drink and a smoke, which is simply a habit; when the Bike's offered so many times before it's a Pavlov's dog type of thing to guess it'll happen again.

One large, full, cracking fucking good pint glass full of Tetley's bitter, responds Mike, nudging his empty glass.

Larry advises the other man who he knows will remain rooted to the spot for the entire evening, Stay put right there and don't move a muscle.

Mike the Bike has this smaller smile he brings out, always accompanied by a nodding of his head.

You all right with the jug or d'you want a straight glass? asks Larry.

Jug. It's winter. It's rattling your bones out there, the wind. Who wants a cold glass in your hand in winter?

Pulling the tap on the Tetley's and staring at the golden column of liquid and feeling the inside of his mouth suddenly as dry as if someone had blown cigarette ash into it, Larry reminds himself, don't take a sip, this is Mike's, think of something else, Larry, anything.

Of course the first thought that pops up, is what a fucking A1 cleavage the woman on the card behind the peanuts has there, enough packets having been sold now to reveal the full glory of a real bra-busting pair of tits buoyant enough to take off altogether if you untied those little strings holding her top on back to front. All that's missing is his very own erection lying there like a sausage between two buns and the whole caboodle happening for real ... but hang on, this isn't a line of thought that's at all helpful.

Drifting back up the bar with the full glass to deliver to Mike, Larry can congratulate himself for having the latter as a regular fan – there he is, an upstanding and physically strong specimen with an immaculate leather jerkin and polished Triumph badge. He counsels himself it's how he should continue to look on his audience however famous he becomes; as individuals each one, the single listener enjoying the same status as the whole.

Standing the glass in front of the Bike, Larry watches as the other man tugs the huge leather book he uses as a wallet from his pocket and ferrets in one side of it for the necessary amount. He appears to be having difficulties and two or three coins arrive on the bar with the value not adding up to a quarter of what's needed.

Patiently, Larry waits. He moves the ashtray adjacent to Mike's pint for his convenience because the latter is a still person and won't want to move an inch more than necessary.

Still digging, Mike asks, You all right, Larry, anyway?

Larry replies, As can be. He chastises himself for staring at the wallet here. Still, with the thirst tickling at his throat, it's all he can do to hang on to his decision.

This very fine figure of a man, Mike the Bike, splendid fellow that he is, fingers two more coins over the bar.

Then he's zipping the purse back up, of all things.

Ta, says Larry, taking the monies to the till and thinking in disbelief, The cheapskate didn't fucking offer, what's gone wrong, was he mugged on the way?

Larry could have said no, it was there ready on his lips, the right answer, he would have refused.

*

Laura is negotiating the cluttered and gloomy basement of
the Dreghorn Castle, moving directly underneath the feet
of the drinkers tramping back and forth to the bar overhead. It's as cold as outside on this 14 February night,
because there's no sort of heating that'll travel downwards
after all.

And the damp – she can smell it.

Feeling for the light switch, Laura's forefinger travels
over the unsealed brickwork and it comes away with a
sample of grit from the sodden surface of this end wall
which holds off the earth, just about, but obviously not the
moisture which is seeping through.

The switch clicks under her finger and the single overhead bulb in its metal skirt carves a slice of light in the
middle part of this space which could be an interrogation
bunker from a movie.

Come on, Larry, she mutters.

A moment later she's stubbing out her cigarette – and
she's going to stub Larry out, she's going to show him the
tester and ask for money: a monthly cheque – no – a
standing order, Larry, let's sort out the practical arrangements, is what this is about.

Her scalp is itching. She readjusts her headband. She
checks the entrances – two arches let into the adjacent part
of the cellar, where the light falls in square or diagonal
cuts, the shadows cast by the brick uprights which support
the floor above.

Was she thinking of demanding a monthly cheque from

Larry just then? She kicks her toe into the concrete, she's that annoyed suddenly to catch herself out. So she's thinking of keeping it despite herself, if she's going to squeeze a monthly cheque from Larry – and talk about blood out of a stone.

She looks at the stacks of boxes, reading Britvic, Schweppes, burnt into the wooden straps. The men trot down here carrying these by hand, whereas the kegs are dropped down the hatch, bouncing on the rolled-up doormats tied together, so they're not damaged.

It's not her head thinking, it's her insides. And this is how it goes, like her ovaries taking over without her even noticing, as though the words come from there, not to mention the behaviour. She hates how it makes her like a magazine article or a problem page letter. Dear So-and-so, I had an abortion when I was eighteen and now I'm maybe having another one.

She curls a fist and knocks it against the side of her head. Anyone home? What's wrong with her in there? Does she feel so guilty that she tries to get pregnant again to cure it? Her body's out of control. Her hair's fallen out because of stress. No, she's not a fucked-up neurotic woman. She's someone who's killed her own child and now maybe she's going to kill the second one. Who wouldn't crack? Someone look after her.

She stands listening to the hum of voices from the bar above. It's eerie, like she's under water; and with the sense of the damp coming off the walls it adds up to the feeling of drowning. The sound of her shoes against the concrete is crisp, gritty.

She advises herself, go back up, forget it, make it tomorrow maybe or the next day when you ask for the cash, when you're not so tearful. The last thing you want to do is cry or be the weak woman in trouble. Tonight, just tell him the news. Let him stew. Then, tomorrow, bleed him dry, when you've got enough stuffing back in you to be angry and cold inside and to take him for the money for the abortion, one hundred per cent.

But she doesn't move, except for a shiver that rattles her from top to toe.

Sex is sex, Larry, she'll tell him, don't fuck with me.

She finds herself walking in a tight circle, out of impatience.

Then, he should stop going on about his wife, shouldn't he? She can never believe it when he talks about his *wife* to *her*. And Laura knows for sure it doesn't happen vice versa. His wife would have the good sense to dump him and walk out of there in a minute if she got to know.

Laura thinks it's her own fault that she's treated this unfairly. She should know married men are never all right, whether they stay married or not. As soon as they cut themselves loose they're walking past you on their way to the next wife and thank you very much for helping them out. If they stay married, then they're still married.

At that moment, she hears a single, ridiculous ha-ha-ha laugh blaring on, cutting through the burble of voices from the bar above her. It rises and falls on the same breath, then it's gone. She feels like it was meant for her to take note, to use the laugh to realise what's happening and change direction. Ha ha ha.

She thinks, people like her, not skinny models but real lookers in a more everyday kind of way, they can have anyone they want on the face of it, but they always end up going for people who treat them badly, as though they hardly exist. It's like, in her eyes, these people seem higher up because they think of themselves only, and don't notice her in the way everyone else does, with full-on attention.

Coming to a stop, she realises she's just walked twice round the walls. She's going mad, patrolling the outskirts of the room trying to get out, her nose bumping against the wall practically, round and round.

Why isn't he coming, hasn't he even noticed she's gone?

Come on, Larry.

She stares at the entrance. She'll hear him on the rickety stairs. He should be on his way. One of his beaten-up old leather moccasins should tread on the bottom step, now, the rest of him following. What's the good of her freezing down here and having to take on Ray's enquiring look when she goes back up, if he doesn't come?

She swears, Larry, I'm going to tell you what you've done to me. It's your business, your fucking affair as well as mine. If you loved me, you'd ask, you'd bother to find out what I was on and why I might not ask you to wear a condom – are you in the dark ages?

She'll count to a hundred and then leave. One, two, three . . .

It's her responsibility – contraception. He thought she was on the pill; why wouldn't he think that. She didn't give any clue that she wasn't. She didn't say hold on or be careful. She hauled him in. She allowed him to take it as fun and games pure and simple, like it wasn't a life or death issue.

Four, five, *six*.

They didn't even talk much, there were only ever bits and pieces. How was he to know she was sailing close to the wind and always had done, her silence like a stifled scream more like, at being a murderer, the accusers held off, if only life could be given even a glimpse of another chance? It would be like a resurrection. The murdered child given another face and body. She couldn't take that away.

And now it's happened, the resurrection, she's going to have to be a murderer again, maybe.

When Larry does eventually come down and finds her and asks what's up, standing in front of her with his sloping shoulders and his shuffling walk, it'll be like popping a balloon, his ego will be deflated that quickly. All that bollocks, Larry, about being able to remember numbers, dropping out from the philosophy degree because the teachers were dumb, playing the ancient music of Ireland that no one's ever heard of, getting the proper, paid radio show for yourself after the crappy pirate station, all that'll be nonsense in the face of this.

Because this particular collision, this accident she's having with him, is going to hit soon. They're skidding towards each other. She knows it's going to happen. He doesn't yet, he's looking the other way. She's in the Escort Turbo, she feels like that, perhaps it should be a nickname. There goes Laura, they call her the Escort Turbo. Let anyone fucking drive. And queuing up, they are. Somewhere in the flash upholstery and fuel injection and the coachwork, she's hidden, and growing colder. Men don't see her, or even attempt to – they just want to get behind the wheel.

Then she hears the squeak of the hinges and the sudden, short-lived increase in noise – music and voices.

It signals that the door to the back is letting someone through.

It's Larry, or it's Ray come to find her.

She moves two paces sideways and drops to her knees and takes a bottle of Tabasco sauce from the cardboard box holding twenty-four, when it was first opened. If it's Ray, she'll say she came down to fetch this for upstairs. He'll believe her. He'll stay for a while and bang on about tanking it with waterproof plaster and turning it into a youth club down here what with the under-the-arches type of feel young people like. She'll listen to him, then they'll walk up together.

The feet on the cellar steps are quick, on their toes, which means Larry not Ray, so she takes the tester from her pocket and holds it ready – it'll be the first thing he sees, because this is what's got to be paid for, Larry, believe it or not, she thinks, waving it like a sword.

Larry is framed suddenly in the archway, a heavy figure

with shoulder-length curly black hair and jeans that are too
tight and those black eyes like coals against the white skin;
with the shelving and the uprights running close to him,
he might be stored in here himself, marked 'singer-entertainer-barman'.

Hello, Larry.

Larry stops dead in his tracks, catching sight of her.
There she is, legs straight as a horse's and her front a
decorous V-shape full of promise he knows for sure, and
she can't be accused of not meeting his eye – what's the
deliberate glare switched on for? he might ask.

He says, dumbly shuffling on the spot, Laura.

Keep me waiting, why don't you.

She seems to be threatening him with a knife or a little
stick type of thing held out in front of her, for some reason.

The truth is . . . he begins.

What? Oh I'd love to know the truth.

I wasn't thinking to see you. I was thinking it was better
to avoid each other wholesale. From now on.

So why d'you come down? asks Laura.

The reason just now is to fetch my amp and drum
machine and my guitar, there.

Larry points to the corner where on a wooden pallet
stands part of his equipment haul, safe from the damp but
the air not dry enough down here to damage the wooden
instruments, as his centrally heated flat would, so it's a big
advantage to having a regular gig at the Dreghorn Castle,
that he can store stuff in here with the mixers, Britvics and
Schweppes and whatnot, only keeping the run-of-the-mill

acoustic at home for practising new material and taking on his weekly jaunt to Talk Radio, now.

A frown creases Laura's face. She says, You saw I'd gone; come on, Larry, this is the routine, isn't it?

Christ, you're right, I know, it has been, in the past that is, a ploy for us to run into each other.

Larry's put his hands on his hips and is shaking his head mournfully because it's true, usually when he ducks down here – as notionally private and out of the way as it is, in the basement – it's that time of the evening when he invites Laura to trot in after him and unbutton her shirt again, as she did that first go they had, as a joke initially, she said later, and it's always been the start of major goings-on between them from that day onwards, 'til now.

So why the fuck are you here, Laura curses, if you want to avoid me?

Larry pegs his fingers in the back pockets of his jeans and gives the honest truth, telling himself to speak very calmly: I was up there in the bar thinking I still needed to fetch the gear for this evening, and so I was on the rack thinking about it, you might say, how to avoid the two of us meeting up as usual, and so I decided to fetch the gear a touch earlier, and while you were absent from your post and wouldn't see me going.

Insulted, Laura asks, So where d'you think I was?

I thought you were in the Ladies there at the end of the corridor. Doing, you know, women's stuff perhaps.

She says sarcastically, Oh really.

The door was closed, Larry explains.

Was it.

Yes, it was. Anyway the outcome was, I told myself I should run down here and fetch out the amp and the drum machine now, before there was any risk.

Outraged, she practically shouts, Risk?

Risk to me, you know, risk to me. Going back on it.

To avoid Laura's painful stare coming at him from the other side of this wretched light bulb which is in his face enough to make him squint, he's keeping his eyes clapped on the musical equipment which stands there waiting on its pallet like a safe station, with this siren Laura in the way – isn't standing between a man and his music a crime, notwithstanding music's the most irritating, cursed thing to be half good at?

But what's going on now, with her arm not threatening him any more, but instead snatched behind her back the very moment he starts forward; is she hiding something? Her position, with her hand tucked out of sight, reminds him of the many times he's tied her up in here, half as much for the joke of pretending to leave her like that after they'd finished the business as anything else – but then the dog in him is panting away and thinking, Hey, the bondage lark, where's the ropes or something, or is the leather belt here round his waist all right; if they've got two minutes they can fuck right now, and with that urge, Larry feels the failure like a weight falling through the middle of him – in just a rash moment the dog can break from its tether and the achievements of the last hour or two will be thrown away.

Like the mixed blessing that music is, it comes to the rescue in the shape of his guitar and combined amp/speaker, which he can fix his mind on – nothing else matters, he tells himself, to an artist of his standing responsible for carrying the torch held by dear old Petrie, hunter and gatherer as he was of old airs from Ireland.

As he takes a second step towards his equipment he's stopped by Laura asking suddenly, and in an overly polite tone, Is your wife pregnant yet?

It's like a bucket of cold water over him – that shocking. He keeps going.

Well, is she?

Nearer to her he replies, Fuck off, Laura.

She ticks him off, saying just the one word but loaded with sarcasm and multiple accusations, Well . . .

Halfway to the equipment et cetera which'll give him something to do with his hands, he fields her a half-lie, We're not started on that road yet, I told you.

Watching him crab sideways in front of her she despises him and presses on, But you told her you want a kiddie, then?

Larry feels a sudden burn of anger at her interfering, he wants for God not to have put a mouth in her face, except for fucking the fillings out of it.

Bristling, he asks, What? not as a question but as a hand-off, hoping to arrive at his stuff finally and escape.

She reminds him, You've told me enough times.

Mind your own.

In her sensible but withdrawn voice she says, It is my business. More than you know, in fact, Larry.

Whenever she strays near his real, human life he could snap her neck.

She repeats, More than you know.

There's a sadness in this conversation, isn't there now? She's shifting a foot back and forth across the concrete. He stops and faces up to her, he should be paying attention.

He asks, So what is it, that I don't know?

She can sense his voice tightening, and it's because she herself is showing some emotion and seriousness; and it's big enough for that actually, Larry, she could tell him, blink and you'll miss it, her sudden powerfulness, because she's that close to walking out for ever and hiding 'til she's past the abortion or the birth, whichever she chooses, and never coming back.

Any weakness in her now, though, will be enough to piss it away, the statement that she's pregnant, make it nothing to him, which somehow diminishes what's inside her, makes it more likely to be an unhappy thing. Her heart breaks at the sudden contradiction – it won't exist.

All this time Larry's waiting to hear whatever it is so now he's prompting her again, saying, Well, why don't you tell me when you're ready. He's more than halfway covered the ground between him and his stash of equipment.

Then Laura is taking the sideways step towards him with that tilt of hers, the white apron around her hips angled first this way and then that, to stop him.

I will, she says, I will tell you.

This human machine – Laura – with the loins and the tricks with its hands sidling towards Larry – all his itchiness about it is the same prompt by good old Mother Nature to have him get inside it, he thinks of it like that since watching a pornographic cartoon in America which featured a clockwork character, it was wound up and then pointed at a cartoon woman and it would just go and do it, not taking no for an answer, its animated cock apparently lifted by a cog and a string and a warning bell attached to it similar in sound to an unmanned British Rail crossing; afterwards the puppet would be immediately exhausted and the bell silent, the joke being that this was the equivalent to the usual male habit of falling asleep so quickly.

Yet this sex trick, to shoo him into having children, is what will ruin the rearing of the kids, exactly that, when he has them eventually; if he's fooled by it then all of them will fall out of their nest, himself and his wife included, and they'll hit a hard surface all right, and not bounce either.

Talking of tricks, Laura has her hands still behind her back, hiding something. Should he ask what it is?

Then she says intently and slowly, You don't know everything about me.

Larry tries for some enthusiasm. He says optimistically, Grand, so what's new?

She's too close, it's when he can see how easy the blouse is to pull apart that he's in real trouble and she's almost against him when he thinks, Christ, don't have the farewell fuck, don't make that mistake, Larry, hold back from the edge, my old mate – but have they even got time for it with Ray upstairs, they've normally finished off and are back at work pretending nothing out of the way's happened by now.

She says flatly, There's things going on inside me you can't see.

Perhaps it's because he's scared to think of Laura's insides in the physical sense, that instead he treats this comment as a change-over to a more elevated, metaphorical subject, so he replies breezily, Christ, true enough, we're all alone at the end of the day, little creatures inside ourselves, to be sure.

Larry is leaning against the shelving, his way having been blocked off; she's folding her arms and making up this amazed face and asking in an unbelieving, sarcastic voice it seems to him, repeating his own phrase, Little creatures inside ourselves?

Because for a moment Laura doesn't know what to say, with this phrase ringing in her head. Then she starts out, mad at him, I don't fucking believe it, you've got a nerve to say that . . . little creatures inside ourselves.

She holds her breath before adding, You're going to be a father, Larry, believe it or fucking not.

Larry kicks off from his post and pushes past her, not raising his voice but trying to contain this encounter within the semblance of a sort of best-friends-now type of feel, it being all over between them, so his tone has this complaining tint in it, Like I say, me and the wife haven't exactly started in on all that, you know, and then he thinks if she can wheel out the sarcasm, he can also, and he adds, So can we tell you when we do throw away the contraceptive devices?

With that he's reached his equipment and he starts to haul the amp off the ground.

Laura interrupts, Wait, fucking wait.

He's loading up his other hand with the guitar.

She goes on, You've talked about it often enough to me, that you're going in that direction, now I'm telling you something.

Larry openly swears now, More's the fucking pity, I realise now, that I treated you as somebody to talk to.

She replies sarcastically, Perhaps you ought to just mention it to her, that you're having an affair at work, for the sake of it.

Jesus Christ.

Larry reaffirms his grip on the guitar and stands there with the dreadful weight of the amp hanging off his right hand, facing up to this nuisance.

He points out, When I was telling you about me and her wanting to get on with having a family maybe, it was just a polite conversation, you know – and now Larry's head bats back and forth like he's watching a tennis match, imitating the conversation they might have – How are you, fine thank you, what's going on, not a lot, what about you, well we're thinking maybe it's time to have kids . . . He stares at her, adding, You can't haul me up for it like . . . I don't know, I've done something wrong.

He's waddling past her with his burden, heading for upstairs.

Drop that fucking guitar! she swears and he feels the blow on his back as he passes her by.

He replies reasonably, Laura, haven't I got to, this is a –

Fucking leave it alone!

He thinks, she must he hurting her hand, hitting him like this. He puts the amp and the guitar case back down and rounds on her.

So what'll I do, Laura, play the frigging spoons?

Then she's lunging forwards and making this stabbing motion and he feels the point of something hard driven into his skull, whatever it is skidding off the surface and not penetrating, but it hurts to buggery and he's scundered.

She's standing back for a while staring at him.

He says, Ow.

Then she's coming towards him again and he's having to defend himself by swatting her hands away from his nether regions, but soon he realises she's not out to rip his balls off as he first thought but she's trying to take something out of his pocket it seems like, he can't imagine what, but she's putting all her weight behind it and he can see the top of her head as she's digging in the side of his trousers, unbalancing him, looking for what? money, door keys? He can't imagine. At first he continues to resist somewhat but when his back's against the wall he lets her get on with it, lifting his arms out of the way, curious even as to what she's up to.

Then he realises it's the opposite, she was putting something in, not taking anything out.

She's taking a pace or two away from him now and looks like she might be about to run off, but the frown stays pasted on her face and she's there to watch what he does.

He dips his hand in his pocket and withdraws a slim, plastic tube with the name Discover Today embossed on the side.

A cold dread fills him. He asks, You're pregnant?

She replies, No, Larry, it's a gift, for you and your wife. Then she's gone.

He can't believe it. Of all the cheek. What a stunt. Does she imagine he'll go home and pretend he's bought it himself and plonk it on the table and say to his wife, I've fetched the kit anyway, love, so let's get down to it? Who does she think she is, will she buy the household tampons next?

Larry throws the tester against the end wall with all his strength and is disappointed it doesn't shatter or make more noise than a click as it knocks against the brickwork.

He watches it drop and disappear behind the shelving.

Then he's picking up his guitar and the amp to make his escape, barging up the cellar steps and back through the door with the Irish football squad pinned to it, the blur of noise and the smoke hitting him anew and Laura there bumping Ray the Landlord sideways with her hip, a signal Larry is meant to see no doubt, telling him look, I can do without you.

But Larry's carrying on, blundering out of the hatchway,

knocking the amp to bits against the woodwork, suddenly gladdened at the sight of his audience who are clapping his arrival; he feels a hand or two on his shoulder as he walks hump-backed with the load, the Marshall cluttering his stride and the guitar under his arm like a gun. He's arrived; the podium is, like, safe.

He turns and signals Ray, let's go.

The Landlord's eyebrows lift and he checks his wristwatch, seeing Larry on the starting block already, because isn't it too early for the first spot? He shoulders his way through the crowd.

Larry watches him, also surveying the hard-drinking public frequenting the Dreghorn Castle tonight from the vantage of his eighteen-inch-high platform.

Then the Landlord's standing with his toes butting against the podium, beckoning for an ear. Larry leans forward.

Isn't it early for your first round? he calls through the noise, tapping his watch.

It is, a touch, replies Larry. His fingers have a tremor in them, he notices, with his hand dangled like that on the neck of the guitar. He closes his fist and thinks of taking a cigarette. He needs to calm down, for sure.

So does it mean you're into a longer break, between? asks Ray.

I thought just a longer first set, explains Larry, to give

the oldsters a turn at the dancing before the young folk come and pogo them to death.

Ray's backing away, nodding his head like it's something confidential they've decided on.

Then suddenly he's bounced back to ask Larry a further question, You all right?

Yeah, why?

Is that blood, there?

Ray's pointing at his forehead and so Larry wipes a hand across his hairline, which is stinging from Laura's attack, and sure enough when he brings it down again there's blood on his fingers.

Oh aye. Knocked myself on the way to the cellar.

Daft bugger, suggests Ray and then he's on his way back to the bar; during the journey he'll be caught here and there like a twig floating downstream, the drinkers who know him tagging his arm to tell a story or two or to win some update on the darts gossip.

Lighting a cigarette and shaping up to tune the guitar, plus every now and again dabbing at his forehead, Larry spies a portion of the glittery top Laura's wearing sticking out from behind one of the uprights supporting the bar infrastructure with its gaudy woodwork and mirrors. She's in conversation with someone, which is unusual for her, and look, they could empty the ashtrays on the floor, pull down the curtains and drain the beer from the kegs on to the cellar floor and they'd probably still get rich giving people their empty glasses back and saying two pounds fifty please, for looking at Laura in that blouse.

Christ, that was a scene, though, wasn't it, no wonder he's shaking like a leaf here. She actually hit him and there was nothing he could do about it. Is the violence going to continue? Should he maybe not leave the podium at all tonight – just carry on singing until she's out of the way? Whatever happens, *who ever shall smite thee on the right cheek, turn to him the other*, hold fast, Larry, you've chosen the wife over the mistresses for now and always, as promised at the wedding and resurrected as a rock-solid, permanent oath on the way to work this evening, but keep your wits about you – no drinking, no visiting the stockroom, no going to the staff bog. That's crowding the goalmouth all right, it's that much of a defence.

Looking out over his audience he's wondering if there's anyone else with such a fight on their hands as he has, which then has him thinking again, Christ, yes, the amount of cocks and fannies in here – and he gives himself a pat on the back, what an achievement it is, so, with Laura looking her best and their having had a row which normally would have progressed to a laying on of hands all right, yet he's got the intact, full scrotum still, he didn't shoot his load.

But then, with his bollocks fuller than ever no doubt after the tussle with his ex-mistress just then, isn't it like walking around carrying a pint: more difficult, an increased danger of spillage, the closer the liquid is to the brim?

He's winding the pegs on his guitar now. Another show, another few quid, an additional listener or so if he's lucky, is what it is, this journey he's on called life, thinks Larry, so here he is travelling along in two minds, one the dog's while the human's is a touch more civilised, or maybe spiritual would be the definition.

Looking at the photograph of himself which adorns the podium here, he realises it doesn't resemble him currently, with his not being able to afford a new set of photos. Cheaper than buying more ten-by-eights would perhaps be to cut his hair shorter again and not use the plectrum and grow his fingernails how they used to be: the left hand trimmed to the quick but all the nails on the other as long as a woman's and built up with layers of nail polish and tissue paper – having to go through that ritual manicure classed him as more of a muso, certainly – and then he'll be back to looking like his photograph.

Now the Landlord's reached the safe station of the bar so there's a terrific banging on the bell and his shouting, Ladies and gentlemen . . . ladies and gentlemen . . . and I'd like to remind everyone he's been working here longer than he's been on that radio show of his – it's Larry Azure!

There's the applause and Larry accepts it but not with his usual grace, his cage has been rattled what with the scene he's just gone through thanks to Laura which makes him think of the Glenn Close movie, the one where she doorsteps the guy's wife and creates mayhem; so perhaps Laura will be after him, following him home to find his address and pushing sanitary towels through the letterbox and so on.

Also, does he deserve this applause that's coming at him, following Ray's announcement? Later maybe when he's walked out of here not needing a collar and lead any more, upright on two legs instead of four – perhaps he ought to soak up the clapping and save it for then. As Job has it, *I am escaped by the skin of my teeth*.

Nevertheless he's a professional so he gives the thumbs-up to Ray who's now swimming back into the crowd and calling, Watch out for your hearts, ladies.

He's aiming to tape up the slot on the jukebox to prevent any unwarranted interruptions from that quarter.

Larry has pulled off his sweater and steps forward, adjusting his shirt and tugging up the trousers which always threaten to drop from the small-boy's behind which hangs below his big-guy's stomach. Concentrate, Larry, he tells himself, shrugging on his guitar again, Laura's gone, say she doesn't exist, you've left her behind, *hombre*, here you are alone with your audience for Christ's sake.

Immediately in front of his small stage there are the more mature folk as usual who are eager enough, God thank their souls, to hang off his every word and dance along to the slower airs, while others playing pool and so on lend him only the most cursory glances and those sometimes hostile; they're having the brightest, most colourful lives and find it difficult to let go and forget they're young and wearing the baggy clothes, some of them obviously under-age, batting back and forth through the doors because some of their friends are still drinking Fanta on the corner – they're the ones Ray wants to open up the youth club for down in the cellar. Larry guesses they are too weaned from this older crowd; they tell themselves dancing in here like this with a man playing folk melodies usually on an amplified guitar but sometimes on an accordion or a fiddle, whatever, is unsuitable for a switched-on young individual who'll want to go into a drug-induced trance, raving.

Nevertheless Larry will reach them later. This first set isn't the thing for serious jigs and revelry.

It's Saint Valentine's night, he begins in a quiet voice.

There's a lady heckler already, saying, Tell my husband, tell him why don't you . . . and she's striking her husband and bullying him, It's Valentine's Day, George!

Some of his fans whistle and cheer because he's smiling at them and they like the talking parts, which is one of the reasons why he decided to concentrate on the pirate radio and not do any more DJing at parties.

But Larry is still itchy; is it his shirt scratching him, or that scene back then with Laura making his skin crawl? There's a throb beating at the crown of his head, from where she struck him.

Fine-tuning his guitar Larry continues, The patron saint of lovers is here with us tonight and is choosing the numbers.

He wows the G-string for a magical sound effect.

More whistles come.

Larry continues, And hopefully getting into my fingers and slowing them down a bit on the frets, later on.

A catcall is heard from Niall who's sitting on his left behind the balustrade which runs each side of the podium; his dog looks up at him sharply at the signal.

Larry tells himself, You're hurrying, remember to keep it slow, you're at the beginning of the first set.

He thumbs the top string and flicks a chord; then as it hangs in the air he begins, Ladies and gentlemen, I was thinking tonight, what is it we've got here exactly – and he closes his fingers on a handful of air – *Life*, you know, with its love and its hate and its men and women, and so on?

He waits for an answer, but it's good news when none arrives and he plays a short contemplative phrase to lead with.

What's it made of, he continues, that's any good? I couldn't find much apart from, let's say in reverse order of importance, food and drink, and music, and love.

I'll have the drink, heckles the woman.

Without even a ghost of a smile Larry goes on to add, after the laughter's died down, Tonight, it's love.

Laura will think he's a shit for trying this romantic line on his audience but she should know he's a different person, this is Larry Azure for real now.

His left hand shapes up to the frets and he's introducing the song, Now this is a very beautiful old melody by a Mr O'Curry, called The Pearl of the White ... and Larry pauses before giving the risky word, Breast.

Saucy Oohs and Aahs come from his audience.

It's a tender little melody, continues Larry, fresh from the eighteenth century, would you believe it, and it'll show you, not all the slow tunes of Old Ireland are sad ones.

As he strolls through this classic song Larry looks over his audience and counts heads, glad that if he can make five couples dance then he will do the same for five hundred or five thousand or five million when his first record comes out. With the music carrying on and his fingers at home on the guitar and the seven couples now – all on the elderly side – slowly moving in circles as though for the express purpose of wearing a hole in the Landlord's carpet here, and counting on the jack on the amp not playing up – its usual conspiracy – since he dismantled it on Sunday, then he can sense the habitual well-being start, anyway, to rise in him like the driving of the head of a pint of stout upwards in the glass; a good song like this calls him, siren-like, and once he's got it off pat and gone one step further to make it his own variation – apologising sideways to the original songster – he'll sink in it, perfect comfort he might say, apart from his fucking irritating lazy left hand, and as surely stirring as if there were a wooden spoon doing it. Unlike some on the circuit he even takes to the clatter of noise in competition with him: the click of the pool table, the sudden cheering at the last double on the darts game and the chatter, all of which he'll mix in as an FX track on certain of his own numbers when he records them.

He's on to the second verse now and the words are going to kill Laura, he knows, and he can feel himself well and truly scundered as he sings, Oh thou blooming milk-white dove, to whom I've given true love, do not ever thus reprove my constancy . . .

Looking down on the couples here with their waltz-type dancing he admires them; they were children once and whatever their characters or deeds so far – terrible divorces, cheatings and violence no doubt – at this point they're admirable, they don't even need, like the youngsters, courage to get up and dance, they are here for just this and will lose nothing by doing so, only gain. The fit between them also is remarkable, out of practice, he supposes; he can watch their feet make the neat, precise movements which keep them machine-like always moving together so it's magical the way they stay tightly connected in the dance, achieving more grace bobbing about like this than when they walk singly to the bar afterwards.

Quite suddenly, moving into the last phrase of the song, Larry has one of the visions he's been enjoying lately; this time it's an imagining of all the dead people who've ever stood on this half-acre of ground in the past sitting up out of the carpet and watching the dance, maybe, or joining in somehow in a harmless way. A moment later he pictures suddenly present all the unborn children who will in the future inherit the jollity here and themselves dance round this square of carpet, not yet conceived but about to be, very nearly, perhaps even tonight; and here they are the quick and the dead and the unborn all enjoying themselves, everyone at one time or another a child, some of the more senior ones having learnt new tricks by now sure enough but still wanting to be cheek to cheek with someone and held.

He'll write a song about it.

*

Now there's a commotion starting up: ribald shouting as well as clapping from the area around the pool table, where there's a handful of seats for spectators of that fine game; and at the same time there's a scattering away of a certain amount of people and it's Tom, the near-blind man who lives in the flats, who'll be causing it; sure enough like he's Moses the ocean separates for him and he can steer a path – his stick a rudder poking out frontways – down which he travels unseeing, collecting on the way the odd heavy hand of encouragement on his shoulder which makes him flinch all right but still he's visibly cheered by it, their shouting and calling, driven on by the whistling of those in the know.

On borrowed time anyway being over seventy, he's a ghostly figure because sightlessness gives him this glide rather than a purposeful walk, his hand and his white stick held out inconspicuously; he's been on the point of falling over for so long now, yet rarely has he actually done so. His teary eyes are bright with drink and the excitement, but upstaged by that conker of a nose, with pores drilled over it and the entire, thin, scored face aimed at the drip on the end; and by the way in which he turns – slowly, moving his whole body and not just his head – you might think he was trying to keep it hanging there.

With the crowd behaving like Tom is coming out of the tunnel at Old Trafford ready for kick-off, Ray the Landlord feels – from his God-like position as boss of this whole concern – sorry that his customers haven't a chance of controlling themselves, they're out to enjoy what they enjoy and don't take into account his bar staff's finer feelings.

Anxiously he checks Laura's position – she's drawing a pint of Ireland's finest, which'll be a long enough wait.

Laura herself, meanwhile, is ready to fend off what she knows is going to happen next: the old guy making a show of himself in front of her.

Tom has been delayed for a moment – by Ray's putting a hand on his arm – but then he's pressed forward by the crowd and Ray ought to know the quickest way of finishing this is to let it happen.

Laura takes up position as far from the hatch as possible and turns her back on the growing crowd of people approaching that quarter of the bar. While she's waiting for the pint to fill up she takes money from a hand reaching towards her, not sure whom it belongs to. She fields the note at the till and gives back change meanwhile listening to the next order, with her head set sideways to hear better and to avoid looking into the man's eyes and having him try to hit on her. With her other ear she can hear Tom's arrival, the old man calling Oooo-ar, ooo-ar, the crowd following him like an echo.

Larry, meanwhile, is a distant observer on the other side of the ruck as he brings his equipment to rest after the first set. He watches the gathering around old Tom and he has this rueful smile about it – there's only a slim chance surely of not growing hair on the backs of his hands when he's in with such a bunch of animals as these, all of them wanting to see Tom make a fool of himself as usual. He wishes he could stay these few inches here above the throng, on his podium, or go outside and walk home in the cold air; what fucking chance does he have crowded by restless humanity like this all fast becoming drunk as skunks, especially with his own craving to join in?

All the while Tom has been making this Ha-chhherrr, ha-chhherrr sound in his throat with a mad grin on his face as he edges closer, interrupting himself with the odd shout aimed at the heavens, Where is she, eh, eh? which is answered with multifarious answers from the crowd, Steady as you go, Hang a right, et cetera. Arriving now at the hatchway, blind Tom checks where he is by dabbing one hand along the edge of the woodwork and from here he'll make his first gesture, offering this spectacle of himself for public consumption as happens quite regularly, bending his knees and straightening them now, of a sudden flicking his right arm upwards and stopping it at the elbow with his other hand, the classic sign for top crumpet, shouting, Harumph!

A cheer goes up from the regulars.

Tom gives a broad smile and prepares to go through the hatch to the working side of the bar.

Laura can feel Ray pass back and forth behind her, half wanting to keep the money flowing into the till but also trying to deal with the situation. The air stirs on the back of her neck, or it's her nerves. He's muttering the usual apology to her, which will drive her mad and stop her from keeping the order of drinks in her head for this round.

She knows there are countless pairs of eyes staring and

people are smiling at her discomfort; the cruelty of it strikes her. Why does she have to be the centre of the universe? For a change she should be the one that's interested, who wants to make a move on someone.

As the glass fills in her hand, she'll have to draw the shamrock in the froth at the top, if she can ignore what's going on.

Tom is singing good-naturedly, For she's a bloody good fellow . . . and his disciples are laughing at his croaky voice getting the words wrong.

She lifts the glass an inch from the plastic grid and squeezes the tap towards the closed position to slow the column of liquid and aim it at the six o'clock position where she'll start engraving Ireland's national symbol.

Meanwhile facing up the length of the bar towards her, Tom finishes his song and shouts, Coo-orrr, you bet! and waves his stick, which earns another round of applause and wolf-whistling and so on.

Moving the glass then, Laura fluffs the decoration, breaking over the edge of the glass.

Is this telling her something – that she can't do it, suddenly? She scrapes off the top of the pint with a knife and tries again.

The Landlord has more or less corralled Tom now and is remonstrating with him in the usual kindly way; a hardline contingent of drinkers with one eye on Laura's embarrassment are doing the opposite, encouraging him, so it's becoming more rowdy, what with Tom giving his call, Fuck-a-duck-a-fuck-a-duckeeee!, repeatedly, his teeth visible and then not, over Ray's shoulder. Not knowing where Laura is exactly, Tom can only address himself towards the loudest of his audience, which makes it seem even more a show for their benefit rather than a message to Laura, and they're laughing.

This time Laura moves the glass too quickly and hasn't the room for the third leaf.

The glass is slippery now and her hands are less steady from concentrating. The noise from Tom's end of the bar is blurring her concentration and she can hear the voice of the man who made the order calling to tell her not to worry, he'll still be drinking it with or without the insignia and it'll be the same, enough to put him under the table, but he won't understand how this might be the last straw, her not being able to engrave this fucking shamrock in the head of a glass of stout when she's 'til now being doing it day in and day out for more than a year, whatever.

With the glee at these goings-on riding high in the minds of the onlookers, Larry includes himself in the crazed glamour of the situation, like all their instincts are suddenly set loose by the old blind man with the licence to indulge in some bad behaviour, and the danger of it like a balloon inflated to bursting point makes Larry ask silently for everyone to calm down, lower the temperature and please, Landlord, take it on yourself to indulge in some crowd control here, given the situation, particularly with the younger members of the pool-playing fraternity pressing inwards, curious about this wrecked pensioner who's making a tit of himself over Laura, and both Tom and

Laura are the two victims in a way, of these hounds who are sniffing around and baying for blood.

Ray is suggesting to Tom now with courtesy and good humour – but in a loud, not to say accusing voice – that Tom's too old to be larking around with the women like this, it's possibly bad for his ticker, so that makes Ray part of the show now and the crowd hush for the next development – what the old guy might say in return.

Heart or no heart, I'll give her a good . . . *ooof!* crows Tom and he begins to unbutton his trousers.

As far as engraving the shamrock goes, it's third time lucky for Laura and she completes it, but then she clips the bottom of the glass on the bar and spills it anyway. She swears, silently, leaning out of the way as though a stiff breeze were blowing from Tom, shaking her head ruefully and attempting to continue having a quiet word or two with her nearest neighbour, out to defuse the situation as always, without retreating and hiding herself away back-stage, which is what she used to do.

With this show going on, Larry's reminded of that child-hood game with the magnetic fish which would all lump together in an instant.

Now then, warns Ray, reaching the point where he'll have to manhandle this fragile, elderly bundle-of-bones type of man back to his pew. It's bad for your health, he repeats, wanting to be gallant and respectful towards the older guy because he recognises that all the men crowding Laura's end of the bar are secretly doing the same as Tom; even Mike the Bike, as motionless as his fourth pint there in front of him, if his self-control switch were turned off, would be giving the same salute but without the humour.

With Laura so sensible, not rising to the bait and remorselessly economical with her reactions as always and carrying on working, Larry reminds himself that he knows nothing about her. There she is with this magical impact on the turnover of the Dreghorn Castle, countless men coming in here who wouldn't otherwise, but she herself shrinks to avoid having this disconcerting effect; even her pull on the cigarette she's just lit is small, diffident.

Ray puts his arm around Tom and begins to move him bodily, lowering his voice to begin repeating, Tom, Tom . . .

No, no, shouts Tom and his hands shoot sideways and he looks like an insect suddenly in an emergency defensive action, clamping himself to the walls and staring outwards, calling, I'm buying Larry a drink, that's what, let me alone, I'm buying Mr Azure a drink!

Tom signals Larry to come over and finish this piece of diplomacy and everyone knows it's done with now; when Tom feels the law's hand on him, he gives up, as long as he's had enough of a show. The audience filters away, the entertainment's over.

Without the music and with Tom subdued and the crowd dispersed, it's suddenly quiet enough to hear yourself speak in the bar of the Dreghorn Castle, although a general murmuring is gathering pace.

It's Tom's moment of privilege – and a thank-you to him for shutting up – to be behind the bar for a moment or two and he has enough coins in his pocket at the end of the day to buy himself three pints of stout and the barman one pint, so this is it, his excuse to be left where he is for a moment or two after his showing off comes to an end, not to be thrown out like a nuisance.

So Larry comes over, ready to indulge in the usual charade, which is pretending to take the money to satisfy Tom he's cut the mustard and afforded to buy a drink for someone whereas in fact the pub itself sponsors him because the same coins are handed back as change – the blind man either not knowing the difference or pretending not to notice.

Reaching this very senior citizen Larry asks, The usual for you, Tom?

Tom registers the familiar voice and smiles and gives his keening laugh before joking, Is that the devil talking? which is what he always says before adding, Yes, go on with ye, the usual.

Then Larry's asking Tom, What's the lowdown? mostly to inform him he's still within earshot if the other man should need to say anything.

The lowdown is, I'm out of hospital, exclaims Tom grimly, his closed fist thumping the bar but it hardly sounds, he's that weak.

In for a service, were you?

What's wrong with me? I ask them, continues Tom as though Larry hadn't spoken. He's playing both parts, doctor and patient, so now he shouts, Your liver, they answer me.

Tom delivers the account of his illness to a fixed spot in

the middle distance like the actors who are asked to play at being blind.

But you're better? prompts Larry.

They told me, don't bother coming back for treatment until you've given up the drinking and smoking, frowns Tom.

So you'll be slowing down a bit, then, on the fags?

Larry enjoys keeping a lookout every night to catch blind Tom stubbing out his cigarettes: having smoked the filter as well practically, he presses the nub down two or three times, screws it down harder still, stirs the ashtray with it for another minute and then drops it. This done, his fingers dab among the ashes for a while, checking there's no embers left and if there's no one to talk to he'll make the search of the ashtray again some minutes later. Larry can picture Tom in his flat worrying about fire and taking such precautions obsessively because he lives alone and is blind.

They put their hands inside me, continues Tom, waving his overcoat back and forth over his chest. They reached right in, and touched my liver, and said it was like a stone.

Not good.

As though it might have been thrown there by a nipper.

Grief, says Larry.

Ossified. Or was it calcified?

Larry suggests, Like in the kettle.

Tom is lifting a handful of coins from his overcoat pocket, sprinkling them on the bar.

Now then, the loot, he's saying.

Larry fingers one coin at a time, counting loud enough

to be heard, until he's made up the purchase price of Tom's drink, except what he's saying doesn't correlate exactly to the value of the coins under his fingers. It's usual to fool Tom like this once during the evening; there are spectators watching for how the goodhearted management and staff of the Dreghorn Castle manage to buy a drink for one of their regulars while making it seem like the opposite is happening.

What about yours? asks Tom.

Larry jokes, *My* liver? It's still working.

Tom's laugh reveals the teeth leaning like the proverbial stones in an old graveyard, and the spittle. His fingers are wobbling. He is enjoying this major outing from his seat to the bar.

No, not your *liver*.

What then?

I meant, a pint or something, for you?

Larry teeters on the brink; what a temptation's here. You're a boy turned away at the door of the sweet shop, Larry, that sad a figure, he tells himself. You've fronted a fight with Laura and managed to carry on and deliver an OK first set without a drink in you, yes, so all's shipshape at the moment, maybe, but carry on in that vein and let the people psychology ride over you, Larry, and you'll miss out on the people altogether and turn yourself into a person standing isolated with no reach for an audience – isn't that likely to be true?

Tom repeats himself, A pint or whatever?

Larry moves a few of the coins back and forth on the

bar for Tom to hear. If this was a normal night and not one he's chosen to adopt sobriety and faithfulness and honour and all those other things the priests bang on about, he'd be pulling the tap on the Guinness right now, probably for the third time; as it is, his throat is dry without it, and he's standing apart from his fellow mortals and frankly feeling sidelined, as though running a more dull life altogether.

Gritting his teeth in the face of such adversity Larry offers a solution.

Tom, that's kind of you, he says. What about if I have an orange juice, can you stretch to that?

Larry's having to shout a little now, what with the background volume creeping up.

Tom's fingers muddle the change on the counter. He says, I don't know; can I?

Larry moves the coins like chequers over the surface of the bar, in an abstract way, purely for the effect. You can, Tom.

Then go on, push the boat out.

Thank you very much, Tom, and here's your leftovers. Larry scoops the coins into his hand and drops them into Tom's palm.

The spectators are nodding their heads; the game's over.

So Tom is pocketing the same amount of money he took out in the first place and he has his pint; and it's only when he's turning round for the return journey that he realises what an improbable thing he might just have heard. He stops and turns back, hoping Larry's still there.

You're on the orange juice? he asks, unbelieving.

It's for my health at the moment, replies Larry.

Not making head nor tail of this nonsense Tom exclaims, A pioneer?

Can you believe it? asks Larry as though there's doctor's orders responsible.

The truth is, Larry's scundered, well and truly; it can't be doing him any good, doesn't he have a duty to join in with the general goodwill and not behave like a pompous do-gooding asshole?

Larry knows the answer very well and he's feverish, wanting so much to lose himself in life as it now presents itself here in the Dreghorn Castle, a festival of fun and drunkenness with everyone mad to get at each other and reach the fucking good time that can be had when exactly the right amount of drink's in your blood and the people around you are who they're meant to be, doubly witty and meaningful as human beings.

As well, the jukebox starts up suddenly, putting a romantic top-spin on the goings-on and recharging the Dreghorn Castle's regulars' determination to be drunk by closing time and the atmosphere of goodwill ups a notch or two, that much louder is the chit-chat so everyone can make themselves heard.

And there's some tomfoolery going on underneath the plastic mistletoe branch resurrected from its Christmas duties which sees someone on their knees with a woman's hand in his hair.

Niall is the next drinker to have fought his way through

the scrum pressing at the bar here and Larry leans forward to take his order.

Black and tan, I'm gasping, says Niall. He wears slacks and a bomber jacket and carries his keys hooked on his belt loop and has the whole Irish package of humour and dark straight hair and self-righteousness and the habit of winking into a glass the moment before it touches his lips. He's an Irishman so traditional that even here in the city he has a hunting dog with him, the lurcher with the darling eyes who'll right now be adjacent to wherever he's sitting, waiting for him on a folded coat, poised and elegant, ready for love seemingly from anyone whether human or another dog.

Coming up, replies Larry.

Maybe it's because the crowd pressing at Niall's back has become so bullish as to make him realise he can't hog a space at the bar indefinitely, but Niall's unfolded his wallet already and prepares to pay the usual amount.

Then he pauses. And one for yourself, Mr Azure? he asks quizzically with the dark Irish hair in several flattened sections around his face.

The hum of voices is suddenly louder around Larry because for the third time tonight he's having a minor difficulty saying no; he can't believe with so much fun going on he should be taking so much trouble to stay out of it.

Larry hears himself complain to Niall, You show me your drunkard's face there with the veins broken all over it, and expect me to have a drink, myself?

It's as though another man's voice is coming out of his mouth.

Niall smiles. I show you my broken face so you won't have a drink – and I can save my money.

Larry holds up his hands as though it's a stick-up in a Western, saying, You've succeeded.

Larry senses Laura trotting past behind him on her way to the till and that gentle breath on the back of his neck is like the first puff of wind signalling the storm, the end of the road, doom and gloom, so with this mournful thought he answers, Seriously, I won't, I'm a pioneer, for the moment.

Christ, on the wagon? Niall looks dismayed.

Larry adds, But I'll thank you for the offer and take you up on it some other day.

Niall's making off through the crowd with his prize drink held close to his chest but he turns round, hearing this; his eyes pop in amusement and he asks, You think there'll be another day?

With that parting jest from Niall, Larry is more than ever left behind.

Larry Azure, teetotal? Christ, what a sadness. It's like, nostalgia – when was the last time he didn't drink? Truly, he can hardly remember; there was a day or two when he had the appendix out and there was a dry spell when he was once too poor and didn't have a job in the bar like now but other than that there hasn't been a call for it in his life, sobriety, not like if he was a tube-train driver or anything, quite the reverse, it's expected of him to lead the field.

He's thinking, perhaps if he's been this good and quick at dumping Laura and signing up for membership of the human race with faithfulness to his wife guaranteed now surely, it's time he ought to test himself under normal circumstances. After all, he's not going to stay away from the stuff for ever and Laura isn't the last sight for sore eyes he's going to come across. The very good Jesus Christ didn't get lost in the wilderness, he deliberately walked in. He, Larry, should have a drink to celebrate and not be a bore on the subject like the reformed smokers who do nothing but open a window at the sight of a cigarette and bang on about how bad for you it is and how they'd never do it again while staring at the cigarette you're lighting up like it's their last meal they're seeing disappear in front of their eyes.

As he's thinking this, standing as he is in the three-person line-up employed to serve the drinkers at the bar of the Dreghorn Castle, Laura's suddenly working close to him and he can see her arm with the lick of sweat on it now.

No, Larry, don't do it.

Moving on to the next customer whom he doesn't know at all, the guy going mad to get his attention and be served next, Larry is lonely in the middle of this crush of people and it's the first time that's happened for sure, by now he's usually anybody's friend.

The guy shouts, but Larry can't understand at all what was said. He curses and leans further towards the man, it seems he has to be that close for anything to get through.

With this tack he's on, isn't he dwindling into a more joyless type of singer-entertainer who doesn't all the way deserve the title of Larry Azure for fuck's sake? Staying sober? He shouldn't be dilly-dallying with such professional ruin, cutting off his nose to spite his face and turning the great Larry Azure into a run-of-the-mill crooner, someone who can't possibly be in touch with the fever building up here in the Dreghorn Castle now.

He gives a cough as he takes the guy's money to the till; Christ, he can't sing anyway with his throat dried out by the cigarette smoke, he'll have to take some water or something, it's his paid job after all, what's the good if he croaks at the microphone in the second set, no one will thank him for that, it's his livelihood at stake here.

And, he tells himself, he's standing at the twin Guinness taps anyway for the other fellow, so why not watch the grand liquid float in the glass now a second time for himself, and there it is easy as pie, his very own glass is filling up, oh so slowly does it pour in, but during the wait he's busy digging in his pockets and putting the required number of coins in the damned fucking till himself, from his own pocket, before striding over to deliver to the other drinker who's waiting on the opposite side of the bar; only then can Larry stand for one moment and ignore the clamour for his services and take his glass – full to the brim – and lift an elbow.

As the glass touches his lip he pauses, holds off, enjoying the luxury foam with a sip or two. He looks at the glass in his hand, tries to shut out the banter and the people calling his name. This is the business.

Then he opens his neck and drains the glass almost in one go. The liquor swims down his throat and the iron-like taste is a homeland: it's Saint Valentine's Day and he's working and taking a drink despite his earlier threat not to. The applause from his first set seems to ring in his ears again, this might be an echo of triumph because it's just that: to have the drink is a victory for good humour over common sense and worry and fear of life; a certain gayness is the order of the day or anyone's spirit would be done for and he's all right, he's done what he said he was going to do; all's O fucking K with the world. Success!

Taking a second draught the pint's completely gone and he has the white moustache.

Laura's flying back and forth with drinks and change and nuts and the ice bucket and a cloth for someone who wants to clean up a spill so she passes Larry every few seconds, but now she notices he has a second pint in his hand pretty much immediately after the first one, so it's the right time to say something, plus she won't easily be overheard above this din. The plan is, some actual communication is required here. He can't be allowed to ignore her for the rest of the evening when she's thrown the book at him like she did, earlier, and yet there's been no genuine word from him so far. She'll tick him off and say when and where the meet will be, then they can start facing up to the situation for real. What his reaction'll be she can't judge, but anything's better than silence. What she wants is a message, a reading of his heart and mind exactly. Communication, Larry, she commands. Get real. Come on, square your shoulders and admit your responsibilities, isn't that what a man is meant to do? Don't leave me in the cold. Fucking communicate. Write a cheque.

With her hurrying back and forth and his joining the fray, now, they're almost colliding square-on; before she sidesteps to go past him she taps one fingernail on the pint glass which he's holding close to his chest and sipping from every few seconds and she asks, delivering the question quite matter-of-factly right into his ear to make sure he hears it right, Now – can – I – make – you – talk – to – me?

Due to the noise and the confusion and the fact he wasn't ready for Laura swinging in like that to speak into his ear from such a close range, Larry is caught off balance, but luckily he's in time to catch Laura's question as it comes to him word by word, clear as day, Now can I make you – torture – me?

Christ! It takes his breath away because yes, some of their best games have involved pain and torture, but after what's gone on this evening between the two of them it makes him angry, the mixed messages she's sending out, and he's confused – can she have meant it? He looks at her and reads it there, yes, she is begging for it, seriously she is, he recognises that trapped look she has, from before.

Larry unwittingly finds himself shouting in reply, Go on, I dare you – feeling he should join in with the spirit of the occasion, treat it lightly.

So, after the anger and the confusion, he's also thrilled by her saying those words and he could do something about it all right beyond enjoying the banter and so on – he can stand and deliver any time any place, he should warn her, she shouldn't make jokes like that when she's dealing with a guy with a hair trigger like he has – what does she want, an accident?

So Larry is already enjoying it, this odd tilt that a couple of pints of stout gives him in terms of outlook: it causes him to see any woman as his rightful property especially with respect to her bumps and her smile and both her legs, whereas his own body belongs to him less when he's in drink, it's something he can give away easily without a single shake of the head worrying about it, and he's dead proud that from previous experience she'll know it's not all mouth and no trousers for gaiety's sake and under his breath he can cheerfully bet a million quid she'd be well and truly satisfied from the roots of her hair to the tips of her blushing toenails such would be the devilish plan he'd concoct, to play at a bit of pretty damn all-out pain and nastiness.

Usual time and place, finishes Laura on her next swoop past – and then she's gone again.

So, she is serious, she is fucking serious, thinks the

speechless Larry Azure – she's bidding to have him back already and it's a big promise she's put down to tempt him. Fuck, he swears under his breath. How's he going to deal with this? Torture, yes, there's a menu for it they've enjoyed already a time or two.

Yet, it's not as though he can't give himself several big thumps on the back for what he's managed so far: well done, Larry, you've kept the dog on the leash, truly you have, look how you've hardly looked at Laura, never mind touched her, count it as the hair shirt, you've pulled it out of the bag, put it on and now you're wearing it, well fucking done, keep it buttoned up.

She can make him fucking torture her, indeed! She should be that lucky, eh?

Just then Laura hurries past him, back the other way, like it's a joust between them but with only her riding, as she hardly breaks her stride to add meaningfully, OK?

Larry wants to get the hell out of here and so with a call to Ray the Landlord that Nature's making itself felt, he scurries from the brightly lit area behind the bar where Laura was prodding at him it seemed every time she passed back and forth and he elbows the door open to the back, letting it drift shut behind him.

And then he comes up short, viewing with some trepidation the corridor in which hang the staff coats and from where his calfskin jacket was stolen.

He advises himself to answer the question, wasn't there a resolution he made tonight, a line drawn on the scuffed carpet here across which he must not pass, with or without

Laura? Only because it leads to the staff toilet, which has a small bolt on the door making it the most dangerous thing on the premises: a private cubicle where, one might say, some very torturous scenes have been played out, indeed they have. To travel down here at all is to negotiate thin ice and he should confess, he doesn't want to fall through, thinking with last-minute, idle confidence he can walk on it with impunity.

His shoulder bumps the wall, telling him his steering's a bit gone – only two pints and he's half pissed already, plus the beer sits in him – his stomach's like a balloon filled with water, he drank it that quickly. Be as quick about having a pee and she won't catch you, he advises himself.

Leaning against the plywood door to the staff toilet he stumbles through and pulls on the light cord and the roar of the fan with its rickety tick-ticking noise accompanies his fumbling at his zip and the distant hum of voices from the bar, muted by the two closed doors between him and them, now. He'll have a quick slash and head back straight away, so.

As he stands there pissing against the white ladies-and-gents staff toilet bowl he remembers where else he saw tiling like this, the white ceramic surface flecked with dirt which has been washed over and over until the grouting's turned grey: he was in court doing the jury service and where the accused stood, a sort of podium not unlike his stage back there in the Dreghorn Castle public bar, had leading from it these white-tiled steps down to the prison, a hole you were dropped into if found guilty by your fellow man. The accused had walked into the courtroom across the carpets like the rest of them but afterwards she'd been taken down the tiled bolthole, shouting and crying against injustice.

All this about torture – what's wrong with his shoes, do they need tying? He bends and unearths his socks, which have gathered in the arches of his feet, and reassembles the whole caboodle. Maybe the itching in his feet will stop now.

Finishing up and heading back to work, with the time perhaps looming for his second set already, Larry marks this dark and oblong corridor, with its shadows and bulky, unknown shapes similar to many a horror motif he's seen in the movies hired from the video store just abutting the Dreghorn Castle, and he waves his suddenly heavy arms and tells himself it's forbidden territory from right now; since he's taken this pee and won't need another until he gets home there'll not be a step taken by him down here, he tells himself. Banish all notions of it, out and do your stuff, Larry, ride the euphoria, give it to your audience, that's where you can get your oats, so, take your dick out on stage with you and use it to win over the general public through and through and then go home to your wife proud and upstanding and chock-a-block full of achievement, that's the way of doing it, forget the long and involved torture scenarios, Larry.

But then, wading through the crowd for his second set, this time with a pint in his hand, Larry feels bad, maybe he put his shoes back on the wrong feet or if not, he tied the laces too tight to cope with all these turns round the knots of people blocking his way, or that tug he gave to each of his socks pulled his toes up; and even when he's reaching the podium there's further discomfort – he drops to his knees to fiddle with the buttons on the amplifier and because his trousers were set low on his waist obviously, that noise was the stitches breaking in the seam running across his backside and when he stands up the imprint of his knee is still embossed, as you might say, in the denim, so he's shaking his leg and pulling at his belt like a mad thing to try and get comfortable. On top of that he's wearing the shirt with the label that scratches the back of his neck, would you believe it. What good is he, as a physical specimen here, sweating now and his hair too long; did the tops of his thighs rub together so much when he was younger or is that a recent thing?

Then he's faced with a short delay while the jukebox plays out. He raises a thumb to Niall who's getting up now to lean over the balustrade and call to him, Did you tell her yet?

Some days previously Niall asked Larry to put in a good word for him with Laura; Niall has the blind hope that he has a chance with her.

Yes, I did that for you, replies Larry; he should advise the other man to polish up his manacles and sort through his whips and ropes.

Niall nods, Thank you, then he sits down, winking at Larry and offering as a final confidence, Watch this space.

On the podium Larry is wired up and tuned and annoyed

with all the problems with his clothing suddenly crowding him for no good reason, but here he is ready to take over when the jukebox runs out of steam.

From playing at the Dreghorn Castle for nigh on two years he knows – judging from the noise, from the Reverend Ian Paisley impersonation going on for too long, from the clamorous voices of people and the number of empty glasses on the tables – that the younger people will want to drown in the music and to dance their socks off, so he cranks up the volume two notches and without a word of explanation, the minute the jukebox ends he bashes out a fucking great chord and swears into the microphone, Get the fucking tables moved out of the way, everyone, there's some fucking serious dancing that needs to be done and we need the room.

This is it, using the anger and the drink in him to good effect: he'll grab his audience by the scruffs of their Irish necks and drag them into excess and deliverance to Bacchus, yes, that's what we need here, he thinks, a bit of Bacchanalia all right, come on, move it.

His public respond with whistling and calls of his name and jeering; they know to take it seriously and they're to have fun now, even if it's only to watch the goings-on. The folk who are in charge of the heavy-set guy in the wheelchair are turning him round and trundling him off to the side and a couple of other groups of people are standing and gathering drinks and handbags ready to shift their tables out of the way.

Christ, that was a good name for his first band when he

was sixteen, wasn't it, Bacchanalia. What's become of the other guys? he wonders. Are they torturing their own women someplace?

He bashes out a third and fourth chord to keep the temperature up, which causes a shout from some quarter and then an elderly gentleman Larry doesn't know is quaintly tippy-toeing across the widening space set now for dancing with his glass floating in front of him like a beloved partner in the little two-step the guy is inventing for everybody's amusement and now Larry thinks, Fuck it, and he's straight in with one of his own mad-dog rants as he calls them, shouting into the microphone double-quick, Let's get this fucking peace process back on the road, can we, all of you write home to your mothers and fathers and brothers and uncles and aunts and tell them Britain doesn't fucking want Ireland, that's the good fucking news, not one sod wants any of it, all we've to do is lay off the fight and they'll give it us gladly, good riddance, but remember the famous saying, will you, that if one poor Irishman is to be roasted then there's another fucking Irishman always to be found to turn the spit, so shall we lay off the gangstering, lay off the killings and the punishments, keep our eyes on the ball for the sake of Christ and I tell you where the ball is now, it's pulling the rug from under the Unionist MPs in Westminster, so the fat sons-of-criminals and perjurers and racists can't have the power they enjoy at the moment in the mother of parliaments, isn't that where we want to aim, because it's obvious, isn't it, we can have back the North if it's not seen to be a climbdown, we've to make it look like a victory for them, d'you see, an electoral victory for them is the business in hand, that's our side of the bargain and we've to deliver it, for fuck's sake!

He's stepping back for a moment, but still holding his finger out to them, pointing at where the rant was booming out to his audience here, who are cheering, mostly. Then he ducks in to finish off, And then we get what we want. A small enough fucking price, eh? And then in two weeks' time no one will care. We'll all be small fry in Europe, won't we?

Sorry about that, there, he says into the microphone, talking through the dying round of applause for his outburst. He is judging it right – the younger people are swaggering towards him and there's a whoop from the backmost corner so now's the time for music and revelry. The drink in him has loosened his fingers, making them more accurate and his voice is no longer self-conscious, it's fired him up to care more about everything, every godforsaken thing whether personal or political, yet to mind less being seen to do so.

The microphone is right in his mouth practically as he starts out on a traditional *planxty* or jig composed by Ireland's last distinguished minstrel in the late seventeenth century, Carolan, which he's transposed himself from the original harp score, speeding it up somewhat; and as the throng broadens beneath him one or two youngsters are pogoing dangerously hard and fast like they do now, their knees bouncing like mad while the rest of the customers are cheerfully walking their tables outwards to make more room for these serious revellers. Larry thrives on this, the electric throne he has here, his voice blown up to ten times its normal size and he's reaching every single ear in the place; something of himself mixed with the entire history and meaning of Irish song is travelling directly into the minds of people and it's so wanted there as to drive them to this frenzy; the floor is full of people young and old and male and female and all moving and shaking their own way; and it's for this shameless response that Larry works as a singer-entertainer.

Larry slides the bolt home, sealing himself and Laura in the cubicle which stands Tardis-like at the end of the corridor.

Suddenly there's no noise except the gurgle of water in the pipes. The toilet is there, an 'O' of surprise it might be, Larry thinks, because he is where he said he wouldn't be, tonight, and in the back of his mind is a grand, emotional apology to his wife and it is a heartfelt one, but his heart is shrouded, obscure, not allowed, *hope deferred maketh the heart sick*. But, he begs his wife, isn't it a glorious type of failure, surely?

Laura is leaning against the wall, her palms laced together over her stomach and her legs crossed.

Larry, she begins in this sensible voice but he interrupts her, Show me your tits for Chrissake, and a surprised, hurt look immediately invades her expression and she lifts both her hands to protect herself but Larry's there first, taking her cross-over top and simply yanking it apart. She exclaims, No! and attempts to hit him but he's raised his left elbow, which stops her forearm, and then he hauls the blouse off her shoulders and pulls it down, effectively pinning her arms to her sides and just with this bit of gameplay he can feel his scrotum tightening to take the strain and there's the added excitement of having sixty-odd people out there in the bar clamouring to see this, one of his favourite views, a full frontal close-up, a great pair of tits nesting in an uplifting bra.

Laura's deadpan face regards his steadfastly and she's saying, Is this your version of talking? If she had her hands free she might have lit a cigarette and taken a pull and flicked the ash, she is seemingly that unconcerned, waiting.

Larry says, Jesus – genuine applause for her cleavage which is smiling at him now, but then all he's done in his entire life is a celebration of the best there is whether it's wine, women or song – and what's wrong with that, he can remember times like these when he's old and sick and won't they make him smile – that was the best fuck we ever had, the night I tried to get rid of her that time, and fucking good fun it was.

He begins to let go of her shirt but immediately senses she'll try and hit him again so he hangs on, tugging the blouse down further and turning her sideways, pinning her to the wall so he has a hand free to run along the back of the bra and find the clip.

Larry, begins Laura, furious with him. Isn't this what's got us into –

No talking, interrupts Larry.

Into all this trouble, finishes Laura.

Feeling the first tweak of an erection now, Larry's reminded of the scene in *Butch Cassidy*, when Robert Redford watches whichever girl's shirt it was hanging undone and he wonders why that picture stays with him for so long, probably because it was one of his first arousals, the same tweak in his twelve-year-old's groin which must be a strange experience for any individual, and the style in which the film was shot, shadowy, quiet, hiding as much as it revealed, leaving him anxious for more – and he can't complain now, he's inches away from it, the very thing, for real; the noise can be heard from the bar, the light is cold and hard on her skin but the surface is perfect.

Larry orders her, Come on, show me more than that, can't you, a man can't live by bread alone, while he's fiddling with her bra strap. Hold on now, I see, it undoes at the front, he adds, spinning her round again to face him.

While Larry uses both hands to separate the clip at the front of her bra Laura is free to do what she wants but she doesn't try and escape, she looks down at his fingers working away and it crosses her mind to hit him again but she feels too sad to do it, the moment has passed. Larry, she begins, calmly. Tell me what you *think*.

Hearing her voice while concentrating on his task, Larry tells himself he should look at her face now and again, a queer guilt overcoming him that he's forgotten it, what colour her eyes are even, and he struggles to remember the details: blue and level, aren't they, straight brows above them, et cetera.

Quickly moving on, he's thinking how the next few minutes are going to be of unparalleled excitement given that he turned her down earlier in the evening so they're both juiced up to the nines; he's that sure of himself to indulge in the sight of her for a moment longer, knowing it'll work, the tension will bring her to the boil all right, isn't he on his all fours now, what a triumph, he's an animal, what with these tactics, it's enough to make anyone's hair fall out.

The clip's undone and he's tearing at the bra and the blouse. The hum of voices from the bar at the other end of the corridor will drive them higher with the fear of discovery, no doubt, bearing in mind they'll be missed by now and some excuse will have to be found, Ray sweating and run off his feet, it being so close to last orders.

He is fixated on Laura's breasts, the loops of flesh suspended by magic, this buoyancy their most important quality: there being no muscle to hold them, it can only be the wanting of the breast itself to escape the shirt however loosely it now hangs, like a theatrical curtain; and to twitch it aside is to reveal a pair of star performers, Larry thinks, their being that eager, the nipples lifted from the ribcage so they're alert, set upwards, the optimism all-important; the word *straining* is used in all the magazines. He can feel his cock answering, beginning to ache as he drops to his knees and puts his face between them.

Laura frowns and puckers her lips, watching Larry begin

work on her breasts and recognising the electric *zing* that flies from each nipple. Also, he's undoing the zip which fastens one side of her leggings. What does this mean? she asks; and seeming to lose her balance she puts out a hand to steady herself on his shoulder. She feels dizzy and as though her breath is leaving.

With her touch on him as he's working away at the zip, Larry is quite suddenly tearful, shaping a sentence in his head as he'll have to, to say goodbye to his wife – I tried, I did, Christ, I tried hard, but I'm into this sort of thing, I have to tell you, yet it was still a grand love between us and I'm dead sorry it's over, it was a feast while it lasted but I've gone backwards now, I'm admitting to myself my true home here sniffing around in the gutter so to speak – and good fun it is too, make no mistake, I'm not disowning it, it's just that I'm not an upright man and that's all there is to it.

Laura is touching his arm and jogs it oddly, and he can see a sweat arrive on her upper lip which flatters him, then he's taken with measuring how soft and round her belly is and the quality grade of her skin compared to his. It's silken to the touch when he places the back of one finger an inch beneath her navel as he stands up, it crossing his mind that she, as well, was a baby once, this button was where a pipe fixed into her, connected to her mother, but it's a thought that has his finger instantly lifting from her skin, because it's not the proper time for allowing she's a woman, he'd rather think of her, so well-built a person and faceless, as a machine turned on a lathe, pretty much of a standard design, polished by hand and still warm, and he's enjoying this the same way he might look at a grand, well-sculpted car pass by in the street with the burble of a high-performance engine all right – and certainly it's not a romantic atmosphere in here, it's that clinical, what with the light being so hard and white and the smell so sour, of cleaners and bleach and whatnot.

Then he remembers it's torture, isn't it, on the menu, so he's taking his belt off and with the buckle clanking in his hands he spins her round to face the wall, taking both her arms and bringing them round behind her and looping the belt round her wrists.

She's breathing harder and all the resistance seems to have gone out of her, but Larry carries on. She's resting her head sideways so her hair curtains her face, leaving her profile obscure against the graffitied wall except Larry can see an eyelid batting like a moth's wing. Is she whispering something, at the same time as she's pushing her rear outwards like this? He fits himself against her, her leggings – although unzipped – still up, and his own trousers also are politely getting in the way – Christ, he can hear his own breath, which is odd after the hullabaloo ringing in his ears from the bar.

He has his hands on her hips in a workmanlike stance and gives them a tug as a trial go: she's willing. He hooks his thumbs into the band of her leggings, lowering them, catching the strangely fragile material of her knickers; before he dives in he wants to see this slope of her haunches, as well maybe as the cleft of her arse and the favourite triangle.

As he pulls a touch harder, he feels her whole body respond downwards with him; he supposes she wants to do it on the floor of the cubicle and this'll be a new trick; and the hard concrete pissed on and cleaned over and over against her perfect and clean skin as well as the obvious truth that she wants it done like this rudely, will make a fantastic fuck all right, it's almost a pity not to share the experience, he ought to trot back to the bar and tip a wink to Niall to follow him back here and join in.

The following moment her whole weight drops so suddenly through his fingers as to knock him off balance before he recovers to save her, partially anyway, from collapsing in a faint, it must be – Christ! He has her one arm and a grip on the belt tying her wrists while her head dangles uselessly, but she's too heavy, he's holding his breath and grunting with the effort of keeping her up so he has to let her drop, slowly, her head knocking dangerously hard against the floor. He calls her name, but it's a strange lack of interest which steals over him now, the very instant that she might be dead or sick or at all troublesome. Laura? He picks locks of hair from her face to see if there are signs of life, which there are, she's murmuring something, he can't hear what?

He asks, Laura?

She's saying, Wait, wait . . . whether to him or to herself he doesn't know but she's twisting her hands in the knot of the belt. Her nakedness suddenly is a medical thing.

He's trying to disentangle her, so he can get the hell out of here, but he can't leave exactly, until he undoes this knot.

At the same time there's the notion that he should carry on regardless and do the business anyway because maybe this is part of the torture scenario, plus he's a four-legged dog and that's what a dog would do.

But although it's a grand opportunity, almost raping her right now, he holds off.

He asks, You all right?

Yes.

She's propped herself up but is staring at the ground, her arms still tied behind her like she's been arrested in a vice-den.

You fainted, did you?

Yes.

He adds in his best doctor's voice, Keep your head down.

Clumsily she turns on to her knees, her head hanging low and she's breathing deeply, Larry more cheerful because he won't have to deal with a death.

He ought to finish unwrapping the belt from around her wrists but as he goes to, he chooses instead to rest an idle hand on the knot, admiring the perfect horseshoe of her rear. This position reminding him of such fucking good times, he takes a moment aside to say sorry to his wife and slots himself into position behind Laura and again tucks his thumbs into the top of her leggings, pulling down. He hears her forehead knock against the floor, a dull thud. Her breathing sounds like a girl's climax anyway as he unhooks his trousers; and with the curse of the damned coming out under his breath everything is there, ready, his cock an exaggeration of itself, loaded. Laura is beginning to sway from side to side, a display. With one hand on the loop of her arms where there should be a handle, maybe, marked 'Pull' and the other holding his cock ready, Larry shakes his head; of a sudden it comes to him what a terrible thing he's doing here, he can practically feel the claws springing from the tips of his fingers and his snout lengthening like in the special effects movies which always seem to have Jack Nicholson in them. To go ahead would leave him finally lost, a real dog, he shouldn't just let go – or should he own up, he is a fucking, laughing hyena, let go of your uptight notions, Larry, of what the path is, that you've taken.

As he pushes forward to be inside her he hears a cry of excitement come from his own lips that might have breathed from hell, it comes from that deep in him – *and so through thy desire thou shalt fall into destruction* – yet at the same time he levers his cock downwards with his other hand, the hand of God maybe like Maradona's during the '86 World Cup, so it's a deliberate miss, he's not inside her at all; folded over her with his chin resting on her back and squeezing her like mad, he urgently swears to himself to stay like that – hold on for fucking grim death, shut everything down, remain long enough, even until falling asleep if necessary, don't worry about her forehead resting on the tiled floor – because it means everything, well done, he could laugh, he really could, because what dog could have done that, deliberately stopped itself from fucking, not a single one walking this fucking earth. God is dog backwards.

The hubbub of the bar is sudden, familiar. A burst of sarcastic applause as well as half a dozen last orders greets Larry's reappearance and Ray is at his shoulder asking, What happened?

Laura fainted, answers Larry, straight away working.

Alarmed, Ray exclaims, No.

So she's just having a breather.

She's all right?

Sure, yes she is now.

There's a forest of arms holding money and empty glasses and there's whistling because last orders were called just as two-thirds of the bar staff went missing.

Over the pitching of the customers Ray calls, Does she want a doctor?

To work more quickly Larry delays answering until he crosses with Ray. No, she'll be back in a bit.

The Landlord's anxious face is right there, hurrying past; he's worried about money – try as he may his sports T-shirt and his goodwill towards his customers are no substitute for her, she's the draw and God willing it's business as usual.

When Laura does come in she's as steady on her feet as you could want.

You all right? asks the Landlord immediately.

Yes.

Go home now, won't you.

I'm OK to finish, it was nothing.

If you're sure.

I am.

Then she's sharing the workload like nothing happened, rushing back and forth but with a straighter face than ever.

Later on, with the doors locked and the revellers finally persuaded to go home, the inside of the pub is so deathly quiet you can hear for the first time the goings-on outside – the shouts, the mad driving, the sirens.

The three of them are working fast to be able to go home.

11.45 p.m.

The singer-entertainer-barman Larry Azure is standing on the step of the Dreghorn Castle public house, happy as Larry for once the apt phrase; he's buzzing with the grand success he's had with finally giving Laura the push back there, no mean achievement which he won for himself by the skin of his teeth sure enough but Christ, how many are there who could turn Laura down at all, what ordinary mortal could have put the stoppers on themselves and done an about-turn, flying in the face of the lust in their grown-up bodies, as he did? He's gleeful; and he might ask this fellow in the raincoat, whoever he is, wandering head down back and forth in the middle of the road as though he's lost a contact lens, could you do it, eh, and the answer would be a sure no if you tasted it in real life, if you were faced with her. The young lad right now driving his moped over the lip of the pavement and directly into the Chinese takeaway where Larry knows it's parked overnight ready for tomorrow's deliveries – what chance would he have had against Laura? None, with his hormones burning away giving him that acne.

Yes, he, Larry Azure, can step up and take the prize for it all right, he's ditched the mistress by a whisker and he won't look back now, he can go on home to the wife walking on his hind legs, a man and a half he feels like at the moment, a solid citizen at peace with himself and it feels rich to have come this far, like the time he gave up smoking – but it's no more and no less than a measure of what's waiting for him at home, isn't it, in terms of excitement and true progress into a meaningful life; it's what's given him the ability to turn his back on the women and not everyone has it at their disposal.

The air is that heavy and wet, it must signal rain.

He steps off the kerb and crosses the road heading through the darkness on the return journey which he generally makes a different route from the one he came on as a diversion, so he can look down different streets and into more windows, pass other people by.

Maybe it'll thunder even, if the earlier wind followed by this sudden stillness tells him anything.

In the quiet, his footsteps tap-tapping, the thought drops into his head as though from the Almighty – Larry, now you'll be a good enough father, go ahead and make the baby, right now, a baby will lock you into where you want to be.

He shivers with the excitement of that. Christ, here's the gap he's levered open with no wee amount of effort, he should make a dash for it and run fast and far enough down this path so he's well and truly in the thick of it – and that means, yes, having a baby.

In the privacy of the first side turning Larry clamps his hand on his wedding tackle and squeezes: his balls are full as can be – because the old engine was fired up a few times all right especially during the last bit of stroking that went on there in the staff toilet and it was never allowed to let off steam, was it, his cock, so even now it's still halfway hard, hopefully to be taken on and dealt with later by his wife – he has the ammunition, that's for certain, and she's at home waiting, he's on the way; the half-hour walk is all that's left between him and fathering his first kiddy, so. What a life!

Exactly, what a life indeed, here he is about to bring exactly that into the swing of things, the power of it in his loins, him squaring up to play God! With a cough the baby will arrive and then it'll be here for good or ill; he shouldn't need another mistress ever again.

Hurry on home, Larry, and collect your prize: a new person!

The thought of it's enough to fill him with godly senti-ments – a baby's not just for Christmas and think what the materials are that go into one growing, for real. Like these paving stones beneath his feet, like the darkened cars canted against the kerb and the lamp-posts marking his route, he or she will exist, but alive with a heart beating and sending out and receiving messages and the stuff he or she will be made of, this infant, will halfways come from him, don't the sperms waiting to do the business carry a coded version of himself as he understands it, a wee building block which repeats itself and gives out a million or two commands as to what should happen next in putting this new personality together?

Yes, godly sentiments, true. Take them by the handful now you're not involved with the mistresses any more.

As he ups the pace a notch or two and cuts through the darkness a bit quicker, the enthusiasm driving him on, Larry's entranced with this new arena he's in and wonders, does the genetic code translate only his physical design and so forth, the shapes of these kneecaps here and his hairline and the colour of his eyes mixed together with hers, or does it mean his thoughts and what's happened to him and what he's done to himself has piled up enough in the fabric of him, as a diamond chappy no doubt but nonetheless with some vices and so on, to be passed on to the infant in some way, to spike the cocktail?

Suddenly he's a touch worried and frowning now at members of his public, darkened shapes, no more, at this time of night, walking or driving past him, all different combinations of race and creed like in any big city, hurrying to their homes or out to a nightclub and the more the pot is stirred, he reckons, the more similar people might all become; after all, to look at the different races from around the world is to see a stone that's rolled and gathered moss, in terms of national character, to make the Japanese more like ants and the English like horses and French more dog-like, and the Irish human.

But with this new life he's earned for himself, the real challenge is – and he's to pick up the Excalibur right away on this one – the happiness factor, isn't it? Providing an infant's bread-and-butter satisfaction with life, even, let alone joy? How would you go about it, except by choosing a partner that's better than you are and perhaps that's the reason people chase lovers who they think are higher up the scale, more clever and funny and rich and so on, to beat out the misery in the human character and push it towards happiness, like an ongoing, full-on effort to cup our hands around the little flame in all of us that only fires occasionally but which gives life its hit all right.

He has no worries on that score, his wife is a plus over him any day, but there is inevitably the questioning of himself and the raking over of his past in order to judge – now the issue of the mistresses is behind him – is he a fit man to have a child in other ways, *the sufferings of the father are visited on the son* and newspapers tell the same story with the tales of incest and abuse and physical violence handed down it seems to him like an inheritance, though not one you're told about in any solicitor's letter but which you've to puzzle out for yourself and can't ever be rid of; this nudges him into quickly examining his own childhood, coming from Belfast as he does, a town with too much God and not enough employment, the joyriders not much more than nippers and despite their own very happy family, when he himself was fourteen years old, only, he and his brothers were doing the cars; one wee colleague aged ten knelt on the car seats to steer, he remembers, while his little brother was on the floor pushing the pedals. They were running with lads from Divis, from Lenadoon, Twinbrook, stealing the cars and wrecking them but it was done to spite the anger and hatred, in the face of suffering, so, yes, doing the cars, he had his foot hard to the floor racing round the flats with the best of them, wrecking and burning while hundreds watched from the ramps and grassy knolls of the housing estates – it was their version of life in the fast lane and they were running a gauntlet with more than two sides: the British Army, the RUC, the IRA, the UDA, the INLA, the UVF and the local community were all chasing them, not to mention the owners of the cars they were taking off with. The IRA were out there like peelers and he himself saw warnings go ignored and then came the kneecappings, everyone asking why they still kept on with their tactics when there were the police and the Army and the IRA and the rest bouncing them in all directions.

So, asking himself in this respect whether he's all right to go ahead and have a child, the answer has to be yes, he had a good family himself to show him it can be done, but then no, he went through the misery and cruelty as well early on, but then again, what with living here in London for so many years, but still living off the greatness of the old country in terms of its airs and good-hearted musical tradition, maybe the cruelty's cleaned off him and he can start again, so, he's able to say finally OK, he'll do it, good enough, carry on!

So, in only a half-hour or so, he'll be allowed, won't he, to have his wife on all fours and there's not a doubt at all in his mind it'll be the best thing, sex that's not just recreational as they say in the magazines but the first spit of life, a joining of them; it'll be heaven, truly, perhaps the only way to reach it and, guess what, after all the fuss, heaven right here on earth, in the end everyone got it wrong, all you have to do to reach that high is to love a woman truly enough to want to make a kiddy together, isn't that the most full-on mix of desire and fulfilment and peace 'n' love, man, and tranquillity and excitement all rolled in one, the tops, the desire alone enough to put him in a trance, into the light of God, somehow – as a baptism-by-desire, because isn't that what the Book teaches, that there's three ways of ascending: by water, by fire and by desire? Larry can't imagine what use the other two ways are – a strange man in a frock sprinkling some water on your forehead when you're too young to know where your own toes are, certainly that doesn't match up and he doesn't fancy the burning much, when you're only deemed worthy after such terrible martyrdom is a mite condescending in his opinion, where's the heaven in that, but by desire, now, he can handle this one, he wouldn't mind at all dying if it's to experience only once an erection that stokes up an actual life, except that's maybe not quite what the church had in mind for a definition of desire, but for him it's the tops.

Stride by stride now he's leaving Laura behind and reminding himself of his wife's green eyes and her exact hourglass shape and the bunch of frizzy red hair tied at the neck to look like a stack of corn in an old-fashioned field except reddened by the sunset instead of coloured gold and the way she scuttles across the ground quicker than you'd think, moving like flies around a light-fitting in the middle of a summer's day with startling changes in direction and all the while accident-proof, like this he pictures his wife going ahead of him through the front door of their flat, and it's the want for her child, exactly this thing, which puts him in the flood of human sentiment, doesn't it, tonight, belonging, a glad participant and of equal rank to most of his fellow men, but which at the same time singles him out as unique, the only man capable of such a thing; Larry alone can want this hard, aim so high and hope to reach the happiness it signals unequivocally, indeed, enough happiness to reach heaven on earth. She's at the end of this walk, isn't she – and he's walking very successfully here, one foot in front of the other, with his wife almost alive and moving in front of him so strongly does he sense the corridor of darkness between them shorter by the minute; she'll be an arm's length ahead, he'll close the gap and pull her towards him, the fit will be practised as they stand like that for a moment and he'll land a small bite on the back of her neck and tell her what to do and it will be immediate, she'll take his hands and hold them to her belly where the button of her jeans will already be twisting in their grip; he'll lift her T-shirt and pullover clear off her head before dropping to his knees while she levers her shoes off, then he'll be ready to work the jeans down her legs leaving her panties awry, impossibly flimsy and on the slant across her behind. She will step out of the jeans and straight away join him at floor level, still facing away from him and tilting forwards to position herself how he likes it, her head sideways on her folded hands, a touch decorous, as if she might be listening for an approaching train but the dip in her back and her knees wide apart making the position a bit ruder than that.

Ladies and gentlemen, if it's going to happen in the hallway as he suspects, nobody will want any foreplay.

It'll be a glory, to hold himself at the gates as it were and yet hold back for a moment to offer a short prayer: please, God, let the old spermatozoa jump far enough and land ready to swim as hard as they can and let the best man win and do the business as laid down by evolution since time unremembered; and then again, pray God the issue of the sex act here be perfect, in other words very like myself – God the Father of all of us, you should be able to understand that wish to see yourself recreated, he thinks. Except that if he was stopped there praying for that long he'd come back to earth to hear her fingers drumming on the hall carpet and her saying don't hang about, Larry, what d'you want me to do, read a magazine while I'm waiting; so then he'd feel himself slide in not wearing anything, in his rightful place, to meet her offering, if that's what'll be happening – Larry has a sudden picture in his head of an egg bumping its way down the inside of a woman; he saw it on a TV programme last weekend.

He says to the wriggler, the one at the front of the queue who's been waiting on red alert all night only to be stood down and then put back on red alert again, he says, we're going to get you out of there.

Promises promises, it says, angry probably with the delay.

No, really, true as anything, just hang on half an hour more, argues Larry.

Make up your mind what I'm doing, it says, turning me on and off like a light bulb.

Listen, Larry adds, when I get to the flat it'll be active service all right, the full monty, no holds barred with a proper job to do at the end of it there, you can go ahead and bury your head in the egg like we've all seen happen on the box.

At last.

And then by some miracle the egg will turn into another Larry Azure, more or less.

Only a few minutes after Larry leaves the Dreghorn Castle, Laura is called out by the toot-toot of a Ford Orion parked on the kerb outside.

So she's tightening her coat and leaving Ray to finish the reckoning, calling goodbye just as the door swings shut behind her and stepping outdoors at the same time as rain breezes down the Crescent falling out of the darkness into the streetlights looking like nails driven slantwise and the thunder is mumbling, still some distance away.

She's thinking, Maybe Larry wants me, maybe he doesn't – and a question mark hangs over her life because this trouble she's in, the same bad mood that's sat on her, won't go away until she knows. The positive result, the blue line on the pregnancy tester, is a turn of events all right, but can she follow it now with another positive result, Larry taking her backstage as it were for the business? Because fuck knows what his angle was, pulling out at the last moment.

She has this cab ride home as a perk on any nights she

works – she's a valuable package, Ray says, he doesn't want men fighting over her like she's a fifty-pound note walking along on two legs in the dark, so the fare was agreed between them as long as Larry didn't get to hear about it and think himself unfairly done by, so she has to wait for him to be clear of the Dreghorn Castle before she phones the cab company.

The air catches at her throat after all the cigarettes she's had; it feels dangerously clean, like it might knock her out with a whole new life here and now.

She knows all the drivers from Capitol Cars. One or other of them always takes her home. Tonight it's Graham; here's his 'Hey eh' he greets her with and she's hurrying across the pavement which is swilled with rain just here because the slope of the pavement's all wrong.

She knows the car interior will be warm and hoovered and smelling of vanilla essence. The No Smoking signs posted on the backs of the seats will tick her off all the way home.

As she opens the rear passenger door she wonders, when Larry tipped her elbow and breathed beer into her face to tell her to meet him out the back, did he ever intend to talk in a – hey, in maybe a grown-up way – about it, or was it always going to be the grunt and groan method of communication?

Then, what was that odd behaviour of his about, not taking her, not sticking it in, finally? Maybe it was guilt. Men – talk about shutting the stable door after the horse has bolted. She tells Larry she's pregnant and then he bothers to stop himself, half thinking about contraception at last.

The terrible truth is, if it's yes, all systems go, the result she's more pleased about is winning Larry, she could take him without the rest.

Sliding across the velour seat and saying hello to Graham she's trying to remember how big would it be now, the growth? She tries to remember. The book showed pictures of a shrimp-sized thing. It'll be alive all right, won't it?

Go see your father, she orders the foetus, and tell him there's a woman here who does, yes, love him, and then come back and tell me what he's thinking, what he feels from top to toe and outside in . . . but only if it's *good news*, she adds, grabbing the handle to pull the door shut, only good news is allowed.

Slam.

Larry's suddenly fucking head-shakingly amazed to find swimming into his mind's eye a picture of this infant, here it is, a newborn, as though dropped in front of him out of this blowy night sky.

He stops in his tracks, attempts to adjust his vision with some blinking and looking to left and right and up and down, but it persists. He turns round on the spot, even, and it stays.

It looks not exactly like him but not unlike him either, round faced, its skin the colour of pastry, with the unblinking stare he's seen coming from babies in the prams trolling about the place, a true vision, floating in front of him so it is, like an hallucination when he was popping the mushrooms all those years ago, it's that powerful a visit. He's amazed – is it the drink doing it?

Even so, it's a signal, isn't it, *and his daughter was made whole from that very hour*.

So he's walking onwards, slowly, not wanting to stare like a madman and have people bump into him, the street that much darker down the bottom end where there isn't any lighting, entranced by the picture of this daughter or son of his with its thumb-sized body wrapped against the cold in its white blanket, when he's further surprised to hear a cry, a cat-like baby's wail – so why isn't its mouth moving?

No, the crying's for real and coming from a house he's that moment passing – he sees the number, 24 – and a light goes on on the first floor just as he slides by and the coincidence of hearing the real baby's bawling so loudly somehow is mixed up with the picture of his own infant that's visiting at the same time and so it's a double whammy, the effect is to have him reeling with the coincidence and general feeling of magic – if it isn't a message from above, what is?

Mixed with this is the immediate sense that it isn't for nothing, the apparition; his prospective son or daughter has something dead serious to say and why not, there's enough in the world to worry about, but then Larry has this feeling of panic because it's his duty to answer the question that's obviously burning up his unborn son or daughter, is what it feels like, and he's a beginner, he doesn't know anything, not how to sing the right nursery rhymes or hold it, even.

What is it? he asks the wee baby.

Its screwed-up expression drops from straining away into the middle distance to encounter him, nearer to hand as he is.

I'm here, Larry says, it's all right. What d'you want? You're wondering if I'm a good enough man? I can safely say there's more than enough of a woman involved as your mother and we're both willing to do the hard work cleaning your nose and taking you about the place and sitting in your room when you're ill; fast forward a few years and it'll hold good, we'll steer you off the wrong drugs and show you how to handle the drink, we'll dodge the illnesses and the accidents and that's just for starters, because there's lots we can offer, like help with getting a job or passing on my ability on the guitar, or whatever other type of happiness can be commanded.

There's no response, which presses him into carrying on, Yes, we're ready to face up to you and throw the dice as to what sort of life the good Lord might give us as a family and we'll have probably enough money and there's a wee bedroom even in the flat at the moment to offer you straight away, so can you tell me, what kind of top-of-the-range infant are you going to be?

There's no answer so perhaps he's not on the right track; anyway if he wants to know what it'll be like, he should scale himself down in size to seven and a half pounds or so and remove all his hair and give himself an empty, starstruck look and he might be part-way there.

Now there's a frown creasing the infant's expression, and Larry hears suddenly – it's asking, Can I come in?

The answer's yes, he says, swelling with pride, Yes.

Is it disappearing from view now, because it understood?

He tries to hold onto the vision, staring like a madman as it fades out of his mind's eye and he's left with reality: gusts of wind are snapping his trousers and he's walking down an ordinary street.

Should he believe what just happened? What's going on here, is God showing a hand?

He looks around, blinking, trying to find the vision again, but he sees nothing except pavement, trees, houses.

Carry on, Larry.

Now he's turning past the new low-rise estate built like a seaside block of flats with balconies and curved, slightly more cheerful walls and outside lights planted like yellow discs along the topmost edge; he's watched them being built over the last two years and now sure enough the first tenants from the housing association have moved in because the odd window is lighted up even before they've finished the fancy railings and the detailing on the top of the cornices, which gives Larry a sense of the hurry in this spreading of lives in the city; we're all rushing to fill each nook and cranny, he thinks.

*

As Laura fixes her seat belt the cab-driver Graham asks in the usual careless way, So how are we?

Without thinking Laura replies, Pregnant.

Wow! Great, says Graham.

Laura corrects him, Hard work, you mean.

After a set of gear changes – and they're in motion now, the conversation is rolling – Graham's cheerful advice is, Ah well, the sickness and stuff will die down all right.

No it's not the sickness, it's just we'd rather not have had a baby so quickly.

Oh, says Graham.

Then she adds, We've hardly had time to get used to each other, you know, as a normal couple.

He asks, Was he pleased, though, when you told him.

In his own way, I think he was, replies Laura.

OK then. All set.

Yeah. Except I'm the one that thinks maybe the baby isn't a good idea so quickly, you know?

There – she came right out and told Graham the whole meat and drink of it, whereas if it were anyone she knew, she'd have clammed up.

Still, there's a long silence between them now and she's grateful for his leaving her alone, since there's a lot for her to carry around at the moment and she's swept up with it, the way the situation hasn't let her go after all, there's still the big question mark over her, it could turn out either way. When she was a teenager she thought she'd be able to duck and dive through life, avoid trouble, move forward, get what she wanted. Now she knows for certain everyone's locked into fate, including her, so she's into the horoscopes and her star hasn't exactly been in the ascendant recently, she can tell anyone that for nothing, but pray God there's hope the tide is turning, because not knowing is worse than anything.

As they pull out of Queen's Crescent, Laura's smoothing her eyebrows and then pressing her fingers upwards into her hairband.

What was it, exactly, that made her hair fall out? Pin it down, Laura, so you can deal with it.

It was because she was having an affair with a married man who didn't belong to her.

Suddenly, she imagines going round and telling everyone when they're together, she and Larry. His folks and her folks will meet each other. Her sister will be rampaging about and doing her laugh that sounds like a scream, for keeping him secret, this guy she's been dating.

She won't care if everyone disapproves. Imagine walking along the road with him. Imagine *holding hands* with Larry Azure. Hey – tell me your real name.

At the same time as this passes through her mind, there he is, the sight of him just clips the edge of her vision through the side window of the minicab and she turns sharply to watch his nodding head with the windblown black curls flouncing around as he walks with his heavy gait; and before the cab rounds the corner she just manages to see the distant figure give a skip and punch the air.

Suddenly she knows it's true: his taking her into the loo for business as usual means he wants to keep her, doesn't it?

Laura leans forward.

Graham?

Yup?

Let me down here, will you, I want to walk.

The car immediately slows. Um, Graham's saying, Er. The car isn't stopping so Laura repeats, I want to walk.

With a jerk Graham pulls over to the kerb and Laura's already halfway out as he's saying, It's not part of the deal, you know, walking home.

Interrupting him she calls, Thanks, and flies back to the junction, her coat flapping in the wind.

Why's she running after Larry? Maybe in the movies it would have been different and, yes, he should have come over and put his arm round her and banged on the bar with his fist and said in his voice he uses to whip people up, Laura and I are getting married, so we are, and we're having a baby straight away, so glasses in the air and toast the three of us, will you – to Laura and myself and the baby – but he's not like that; and so what happened, that's his version of saying to her, let's you and me carry on? The big baby, himself!

Approaching the corner, Laura slows and tucks one side of her hair behind her ear. They'll bump into each other, face to face. It worries her what she'll say to explain that – she can't pretend it's an accident. I saw you from the cab, Larry – tell the truth for a change and from now on, always.

Then she has the full view of all four roads and she stands and scouts for the familiar figure, but she doesn't immediately find it; and when she does, a frown crosses her expression because it's a rear three-quarter view of him some distance away still, as he's just swinging out of sight into a paved alleyway with the iron framework set across it to prevent cyclists from speeding through – and so he won't come this way at all.

She hesitates. The alley is frightening and he'll have reached the other end of it by the time she gets there, so maybe she shouldn't follow.

Plus, is it ladylike to run after your man through the rain?

She won't see him 'til next week though – and she doesn't have his number.

Maybe he'll break the habit of a lifetime and phone her at the pub during the week.

A voice interrupts from some distance away, calling, Laura. Surprised, she sees Graham in his car with his elbow out of the driver's window, holding two crooked fingers towards her. He's saying, It's not part of the deal, is it, for you to walk home.

She insists, I'm all right, thanks, I'm walking, and she heads off.

*

Larry enjoys a brief tussle with the metal hoops welded into the end of the alley here to prevent skateboarders whizzing through – and passes into Talacre Road now. Drops of rain are knocking on his shoulders, so heavy as to sound like insects crashing into the light shade. A shiver starts at the back of his neck and he turns up his collar, walking a touch faster.

He had a vision back there – so does this make him up for sainthood, already? It's disappeared right now, but he's more than ever convinced it was for real, a miracle, and he didn't want to shake off the wee visitor, there was a lot of blinking going on in quick succession for a while to try and keep hold of it. He's that disappointed, he's making up his own picture of his future child, but a touch older, because fenced off from the old railway siding on his left is the patch of grass used by other people's kids as a playground and by the dogs as a toilet and it's a surreal scene: a blue milk crate tinted with orange from the sodium streetlights is hanging from a length of cable suspended between a tree and a lamp-post; the tree has all its lower branches broken, it wears this thin and ghostly skirt of dead boughs where a pack of kids have obviously climbed up time after time. The game is, he guesses, the trainee vandals hold on to the crate and slide down; it's like their assault course and by the look of it they've played it to death here.

And this is the sort of thing you'll be up to in your first dozen or so years of your life, Larry tells his firstborn, now grown in his mind's eye to a five-year-old. It's brilliant, isn't it, think of it, you'll be like these children playing here again tomorrow maybe with the crate and the tree and so on, and that's what life'll be for you, the activity, the goings-on, the in-and-out breaths, the running around in circles, the queuing up at the tree there, the climbing up and getting hold of the milk crate and casting yourself off for the ride back down to the ground, the friction of the milk crate on the rope or cable it looks like, which would be slowing you down. You'll have to climb the tree again, which is more difficult now all the branches have broken off. You'll gash your knees and twist your back and get yourself ticked off by your ma for general rioting, but it's the life, what you'll be up to; it might change by the time you get here but it's life with a capital 'L', isn't it, and let me tell you it's not much different when you're an adult, come to that.

He pictures his five-year-old son or daughter running at his feet and explains to the child, Understand then, what'll be yours to call your own and give thanks for – so without delay seize on it and join us if you can – is, yes, Life; that's all I can promise, I can't even say it will be a long or healthy one but it isn't a nothing answer exactly, is it, it's no mean thing.

Right now for your father you might be interested to know that it's the smell of the wet city air and the knocking of his heels on the ground and the inside of his own head, carried as it is every waking moment on his shoulders, and you're all right as long as you don't too often go near the cliff edge which looms up pretty suddenly if you scrabble around too much in your own nest hoping to try and work anything out as to what things mean exactly.

Larry has the strange sensation, now, that for each of his footfalls there's another, slighter one echoing it and he judges it must be the raindrops splatting against the paving stones. It's adding up to a ghostly walk home, tonight, in more ways than one.

Then his thoughtful five-year-old – perhaps with a sprinkling of freckles, like its mother – will no doubt ask the polite question, Are you sure, Da, it'll be all right, the Life thing, if it's given from you, particularly? Don't forget there's someone else involved and that's my good self; with your well-advanced plans for my arrival what have you got to offer exactly, that makes it such a grand idea?

Christ, look at the trouble the wee thing is causing me already, thinks Larry but at the same time he's proud to the bottom of his boots, it's going to happen, *narrow is the way which leadeth unto life, and few there be that find it.*

Larry has a tear in his eye and his footsteps aren't all the way in a straight line on the pavement here, he's weaving from side to side among the puddles now appearing on the ground, raindrops falling that far apart and of a large enough size to look like God's opening the taps all right and planning a proper storm.

Wobbling like this, he should query how many pints he knocked back in the Dreghorn Castle just now, to be so tottery on his feet and to volunteer for this imaginary question-and-answer session with his unborn son or daughter – and be truthful now, he advises.

Enough pints, is the answer. Carry on, Larry, and sober up as you go, no more imaginings, just the one foot in front of the other.

Larry gives himself more of the same encouragement, Come on. Hurry.

He hears a child's voice then calling him from some distance away, Larry.

So the weirdness isn't over yet tonight, with the footsteps and the voice he's sure he just heard for real.

I'm coming, he answers in his head – but maybe the words were spoken out loud here, which means other pedestrians will think he's mad talking to himself as he goes along, he should tell everyone he's on his guard with this important interview going on with his firstborn and he has to give it something to look forward to or the whole thing's up the spout maybe, if it can refuse to start out on the journey on the grounds of there not being enough on offer.

He feels a stir of cold air on his neck – what is it – dread that the child will accuse him of negligence and cruelty if he's not a good enough man.

So he begins to jog along a bit faster through this noisy, wet February night with the raindrops still falling – *splat* – big as bird-droppings every now and again; and he thinks about how difficult it's been to do what he's wanted in life because there've been so many others after doing the same thing: the singing, the DJ work, and everything to do with his crowded profession, showbusiness.

But then, he is a success in his own terms, he has his lady and the acoustic guitar at home and his own songs building to a pretty ace collection, plus the graveyard slot on Talk Radio after slaving away at the pirate radio for years and so he could say he has an individual talent – no one else could take up doing this, not in exactly the same way, he's carved a territory without realising it; like water scouring a rock that stands in the way of a stream, a life can wear a hole for itself of a particular shape and that's all there is to it, as sure as he's putting the one foot after the other right now . . . a prime-time slot with a national radio station will be the next rung of the ladder and he's allowed to dream there'll be room for him to move up a notch or two in terms of his professional life.

He trots on blindly, his eyes literally closed for a moment against the rain that's fringing his eyelashes now, the pavement in front of him stretching far enough so as not to have him worry about where he's going and there, his firstborn child is a teenager now, stronger than ever, long hair, moody as hell and asking the next important question, Is there room for me, Da? Any space left at all with all those other folk crowding in, there? And then it's looking a touch intrigued, it can be said, at what its da has come up with as an answer: yes, life at the moment has a spare corner or two. You can look forward to making something of yourself, he offers, you can become a disc jockey or a musician or a builder or a something, a barman say, or a lawyer or a teacher, just by doing it often enough and for a long enough time, normally speaking. The white Ford Escort van Larry's passing by here has a roofrack with a plumbers' tube mounted on it for carrying the copper piping and there in the driving seat will tomorrow morning sit the man who's plumbed often enough to become a plumber, whether a good or bad one is a definition; you become what you do.

And then Larry's falling, literally – having blundered into a stash of bin-bags lying out at the bottom of the street, he's pitched headlong and rolls in the rubbish, opening his eyes and accusing himself, You drunken bastard, get up, but the world is spinning a touch more than it should and it's a moment or two before he finds solid ground by pawing his way out from the mess and only then managing to lever himself upright, cursing.

Out of the corner of his eye Larry glimpses an abrupt movement behind him and he thinks, Sorry, he must have scared someone and they're veering away, avoiding him. Honest, I'm not a violent rapist, relax, I'm only one over the odds.

Also, there's a twitch of the curtains now in the window of the house he's walking past, which tells him people were watching as he rolled around in the gutter like a drunk.

He has to laugh, what was he doing with his eyes closed for so long, what did he expect? It's lucky he didn't stray off the pavement and get hit by a car.

He bats at his clothes expecting to find grime and food

deposits but they're none the worse, he's survived the wee
accident here – except he's wet from the rain.

Less talking and more walking, he counsels himself.

So yes, he says to the sixteen-year-old youth who's wearing Larry's own face but youthful, renewed as if by magic
there in front of him, despite appearances with your father
falling over, there's enough room for you.

Then it occurs to him it might be a girl – in which case
watch out for the men, let your father advise you.

Because the rain is heavier Larry shivers and puts on an
extra turn of speed to reach some decent cover and after a
while he gains the overhang of a railway bridge here, so
he sidesteps quickly and stays put, looking upwards to judge
the rain of that blustery type which although heavy might
disappear as quickly as it came.

Trotting towards him down Prince of Wales Road is a
pretty enough woman, he'd guess, a fellow sufferer wanting
to be out of the rain and it's because she's looking for a taxi
that she's stopping to look up the sidestreets and turning in
each direction, a touch bewildered – don't taxis always
dissolve in the wet, he'd suggest.

Or is she lost?

Glancing beyond her, Larry can just spy the notorious
safe haven and all-round good pub on the corner there,
the Fiddler's Elbow, whose curtains are drawn so tightly he
suspects the inmates are carrying on a little later than the
law gives licence for. He considers advising the woman
they should both head up there to enjoy a whiskey and
wait out the rain, just as a harmless flirtation, a moment

or two's conversation, no more, he's beyond looking for a mistress any more, ever.

It's a grand idea all right, he's played often in the Elbow with the fiddlers *en masse* and they are a committed type, what with the sawing like fury at their instruments and their carrying on in general with women and drink and the odd row or gambling scandal: some fine nights have passed around the ale-soaked tables. So why not?

She'd probably say no; she'd be scared of him, looming out of the rain as he would. She'd think it was going to be another roadside murder of a damsel in distress.

Apart from the girl looking for the cab there are a few more figures dotted about the pavements now: young men hurrying singly or pitching drunkenly in threes, suddenly, as though all the pubs have just emptied to this spot, and the cars of course are screaming past all dark on the inside enclosing the fragile lives and sharp with lights and reflective paintwork on the outside.

And then he imagines it's his eighteen-year-old daughter standing in the rain over there, not able to afford a taxi. I tell you what, suggests Larry, I'll buy you a mobile phone as long as you promise only to use it in emergencies, not for the general toing and froing of your social life, and I can be there quick as a flash anywhere in the London area, or I'll send the limo for you.

He'd swoop by and pick her up and they'd settle back against the leather upholstery and he'd say, Think of it like this, you get your own storybook, with pictures – your life as can be had by not a single other person, which is almost to say it's your duty to come and do it as best you can according to your fate, isn't it?

Waiting, Larry instructs himself to try and plant in his memory this exact moment – now, as he stands and observes how the shadows hide in patches away from the streetlights, as he watches the interior of the house opposite with strangers walking back and forth lit by the blue flickering of a television screen, as he observes the ghost of his daughter over there who's given up standing in the rain and is walking in his direction still craning her neck for sight of a cab, right *now* – as one of the happiest in his life because that first vision and afterwards this wide-ranging interview with his firstborn aged nought all the way up to eighteen during the walk home from the Dreghorn Castle is no more and no less than a very active contemplation of fathering someone; he's swooning just at the thought of his success.

When he or she is eighteen, Larry won't be working at the Dreghorn Castle any more, instead he'll be remembering it as somewhere he used to work; and he craves the knowledge of what he'll be up to then, exactly which radio station and which slot he'll be on.

Taken with the notion of imagining himself further and further in the future it follows the time'll come when he won't be working at all, he'll be old and retired and even the many radio stations he's worked at will be a memory only, as was the Fiddler's Elbow just now, so he can tell his first son or daughter, join in, will you, it's up for grabs all this is.

He adds finally and emphatically, I want to see how you'll turn out, is the long and short of it.

And then the rain is calming suddenly – and it's quieter, thank Christ, the wind is dropping a touch and now he can enjoy the phrasing of this number he's playing in his head, not so much a song as a *parlante* accompanied by Yeats' lady, Florence Farr, on her famous psaltery, the words going something like, *when the wind has sung, the lonely of heart must wither away*, and like all soul numbers, isn't it going straight in and finding the human heart as it always does, so let no one switch off or change stations, you might be working the nightshift at a bakers' shop or perhaps you're listening via a satellite hanging in space with a 'footprint' as they say reaching halfway round the world, or perhaps you're in a quiet room with your whole family surrounding you in other rooms, asleep in a foreign capital, but whichever's the case, go on and take pride in your listening, it's something difficult, anyone can be proud of listening well.

Then there's the sinister, distant thunder murmuring in the sky.

At the same time, Larry's concentration is broken and he jumps out of his skin because he recognises her: the girl who all this time has been making sporadic progress towards him is Laura – and he was picturing her as his daughter, for Chrissake, show me the guy who's been messing you around in that pub and I'll give him a hiding all right.

Laura.

It's enough to make his mouth dry on the spot but he manages not to betray himself, he doesn't move an inch; and he can see by the way she's been stopping and starting and staring in all directions that she hasn't seen him yet although she's bound to. Larry might stick to his guess that she's looking for a taxi instead of waiting for a night bus, which would account for why she's had to walk so far already from the pub without finding one.

He doesn't know whether to break for it and run, hoping she doesn't recognise him from the back view, or maybe he should stand stock-still in the shadow here under the bridge and hope she won't see him, or perhaps, should he step from the shadows and enjoy frightening the life out of her? Because sure enough his own heart is skidding along.

Already he's too late to move because she's that near, he'd frighten her into noticing him, plus, whatever he said to explain it, wouldn't she know that either he was avoiding her, or that he was lying in wait?

By the time he's dawdled through these few plans of action, she's on him – and so close he could take a step or two and touch her shoulder. She walks past wearing an intense expression – he would guess it's due to the frustration, what with straining your eyes for the only cab in London with its light on tonight. Then the danger is over and he's behind her, watching her proceed steadily into the wind and he feels relief.

Just as Larry is making up his mind to move off from the shelter of the bridge and continue his journey home, he hears the crash of gears and a car he's seen twice before zooming back and forth tears past again – and this time, with a squeak from its front tyres, it pulls up alongside Laura.

She keeps walking, so the car idles along, kerb-crawling. Larry observes her throw a comment or two sideways into the car window which is at this moment jerkily being wound lower.

Seeing this, Larry fears for her, although it's likely she'll be able to see this guy off the premises as it were and the fellow will, probably, take fuck off for an answer, with no hard feelings, if he's just a bit sporting with the women and not a maniac. Nevertheless, isn't it the done thing for Larry to be a hero and make sure she's safe because the kerb-crawler, no more than bothering her at the moment, might get out of his car and force her into an alley or suchlike and there's hardly a soul around that'll help her.

Following them, Larry sees her pause increasingly often and talk into the car; it seems like she's not too angry, merely asking him to drive on, which is probably the sensible approach.

Observing such a thing happen in front of him to someone he knows intimately is enough to give Larry the sense of what the women have to put up with, for the sake of Christ, from every direction and out of the blue as well, obviously. He shakes his head, tut tut.

Then Larry's stopped in his tracks because Laura's opened the rear passenger door and stepped into the car.

The brake lights switch off and the driver very sedately pulls away, taking her with him. Larry's gobsmacked.

Laura watches the back of Graham's neck which is motionless, it's just his hands on the wheel moving the car this way and that, his head is steadfast, the shoulders square and looking too strong. She thinks, It's over. Hasn't she had enough of beating her head against a brick wall, doesn't she know for certain that Larry's a drunk – look at his falling over just now – plus he's a liar and a fake. Isn't a couple of years long enough to find that out and stop herself from inventing the idea that it's ever going to be different?

She tries it out, thinking, Larry, you're a drunk bastard who falls over in the street and I was dreaming, thinking it might be OK. I am full of hate for you and if you were here I'd tear your fucking eyes out for even looking at me in the first place and I want you to know that my heart is broken, there's not one good bit of it left, it's hard as stone now, from loving a sad old fucker like you.

She presses her hands harder into her belly. It's probably just some straightforward girl who'd get married and work at something, growing in there, someone like her, so she won't be missed. No loss to society. If it's a boy, it's her duty, no more Larry fucking Azures please, do the human race a favour.

Certainly, she's going to decide whether or not to get rid of it by the end of this journey.

She closes her eyes for a moment to imagine, if it was a girl, she might be a top model or an actress.

She opens her eyes again to observe Graham craning his neck to see out of the junction, before taking off. She can tell he's proud of himself, sticking to his job, hunting her down like that, getting her home. Isn't a male the most protective thing, she offers as a final irony.

This journey: the five set tones of the engine and the back of this Graham's head, the other cars buzzing around, the roundabouts and lights and the criss-cross of roads, lined with house after house and whole blocks of concrete and brick crammed with flats. How many trips in cars are there, with people bouncing off the walls of their living rooms and walking back and forth on the streets all night, some of them to go to the Dreghorn Castle and be served by her, a dot of a person as meaningful as any other and inside that dot, a smaller one, both of them infected with this *hatred* of Larry Azure, whoever he is.

It's sad, all types of people are rattling around for any number of reasons, each person making only a bit of a difference to one or two others' lives, eating and sleeping and fucking and watching TV pretty well all the time, scraping livings to share out between them. She had a part-time job doing the census once and it's like that now, seeing everyone as numbers, more piled on more, lots of biro marks, and all the forms she collected read the same but different, the world like an ant-heap, but with all the ants unique individuals, precious and not replaceable, thinks Laura, but only in their own eyes.

Laura judges it shouldn't make a difference whether Larry's alive, a tick on the census form, or not. She's alone with this. Larry's a married man and a drunk.

The Ford Orion is in Kilburn High Road now, which is crowded even at night; the pavement can hardly fit another person on it outside the Bricklayers Arms here.

She takes a strand of fake hair and curls it in her fingers, smoothing and twisting it needlessly. She picks at cuticles, digging out shards of skin and peeling them back until they're raw – again.

Larry fucking Azure, Mr *False Name* – what other sign does she need – because what she wants is an omen, right now as she sits soaked with the rain and holding her stomach and wishing it didn't exist, this ache.

Through the smell of vanilla she can tell there's cigarette smoke in her clothes and hair.

Now she presses harder into her abdomen with her fingers. She's thinking, God, the penalties of having sex, for a woman.

She wants to say sorry to the foetus. If she gives it a name and apologises it'll be what happened before. Also she remembers having these thoughts: its spiritual life is in her hands, she should have it baptised.

There's tears in her eyes now at how impossible it is to make a decision. She can say yes and the next minute she wants to be pro-life and look after it for ever. What will allow her to say yes or no, by the time she arrives home, what will tip the balance? There is the deadline anyway: twelve weeks, or is it sixteen? After that she'd have to drink and take drugs and throw herself downstairs like they had to before legalisation. So it sounds like another typical Saturday night out, then.

She may as well stick to her own deadline, to decide by the time she steps out of Graham's Orion, or the toing and froing will go on for ever.

Does it feel the pull of these corners?

Graham is braking sharply. In the middle of the road a tramp has stopped, knees bent, raising his arms and shaking both fists in the air before clawing at his own face and continuing to stagger across the road. Graham doesn't say a word, he drives on without even looking sideways to follow the man's progress but Laura does, because there goes Larry Azure in twenty years' time, for certain, and that'll tell her which way to jump. He's ruined her life both financially and emotionally, that tramp Larry Azure, God save her from him, fight now, Laura, and be done with it, hoover it out, the baby can be thought of as someone hunting her down, it wants to steal her life and ruin her even more. For each year added to the baby's life she can subtract a certain amount of spiritual well-being and self-respect and financial security from her own.

Just here then, she reminds Graham. Her voice sounds surprisingly normal.

It's the usual corner; he knows to swing round and drop her on the other side of the road.

As she uncrosses her legs to climb out of the car she

tells herself not to be stupid, what sign does she need – don't do it, Laura, she tells herself.

These thoughts – when she's simply asking Graham for a receipt for the fare, the sound of her voice comes out sounding desperate, like it's an emergency, The receipt please.

Stepping away from the car she looks down and sees a child's shoe lying in the gutter, just the one, soaked with rain and the laces missing.

The very famous Larry Azure is running now full pelt and his lungs are puffing in time with the slap of his shoes on the streaming pavement and the streetlights come and go one by one, fighting off the darkness, but he's happy, isn't this something, to be running through a heavy Saint Valentine's night storm for a serious ronday-voo with his missus as he is, and he's glad still to be able to run at all given the state he's in – although his breathing's harder now, he's not sure he can keep it up all the way.

What was all that about with Laura and the kerb-crawler? Larry asks himself, because he's a hundred per cent certain she's not the type to have gone in a bloke's motor at the drop of a hat. No, what he witnessed was for sure, an undercover policeman working on clearing prostitutes from the streets or something, offering her a lift home. Or a boyfriend – yes, maybe there was a lover that picked her up from work and they fought and she jumped out and he raced round looking for her and then she hopped back in.

So there's someone else she can go to, she's not left high and dry at all, which is soothing.

He slows to a walk, his heart thudding. Then it gives, like, a little triple jump, and he's frightened it's an early heart attack so he stops and leans his hands on his knees, to recover his breath. Suddenly, he knows he won't ever go back to the Dreghorn Castle. That was his last gig he did there tonight. It's halfway gone, is the overdraft, and he's on to his new life already. He'll call Ray the Landlord and give him the news and of course answer yes to the query will he, Larry, come back and have a pint and shake hands for a goodbye and at the same time pick up his gear. Larry shakes his head and the wet curls tickle his brow. What a set of musical chairs tonight: Laura off with her new man, while he's now swapped over and is *on the path less travelled*, but steady as she goes and all views fair, is his hope.

Near to the end of his journey now, he resumes his walk and shrinks as much as he can into the collar of his jacket as he makes the last few uphill steps against the rain before turning into his road to be gladdened – as he is every day – by the fact that his flat is in a 1930s block and not a '60s one when they started in on using the concrete as a building material; he knows to his family's cost what that did to the bricklaying trade as his grandfather and father were both seasonal brickies over here for the summer building spree and then back home for wintering with their families.

What did his ancestors do for women when they were

away all summer long? Larry wonders, because isn't it true that men think of sex every couple of minutes and Larry reckons this is the minimum, surely it's every three or four seconds or so, that must be more the norm. No doubt they were beating their salamis back at the lodgings in Kilburn or wherever the community was.

Christ, he swears, admiring the contours of his block easy as it is on the eye like a mansion, what the fuck has concrete done, it's taken the guts out of people's homes, massacred the streets, it has.

There can be no doubt he's on for a go with his lady tonight. Maybe it's the action of his legs back and forth while he was running that's rubbed him up the right way, which is a bit of a head start for his missus you might say, helping her along, because even now his cock is inching its way down his right-hand trouser leg after its brief rest during the middle part of his walk. So is this the same erection or a new one? he wonders; it's difficult to tell when even slipping the key into the lock of the new metal door here – one of a set guarding all the stairwells now due to thieves making use of the rabbit-warren type arrangement for easy pickings – when even this simple in-out action of the male key and the female barrel is a turn-on.

He'll choose to say it's the very same erection with the same wriggler first in the queue keen to disembark, no practice run this, waiting its turn like in the Woody Allen movie and a proper job to do, a wee life to kick-start, a lot of responsibility.

Calm down, Larry advises himself, what's to say his wife is feeling like it. Don't build your hopes, Larry.

She'll see his point of view, though, when he tells her about the excitement of the homeward journey with the weird vision and his gun likely to go off at the thought of a woman or even just the sight of them on the advertising hoardings. He could get lost in the beauties on the posters; what'd it be worth to pillage them for hours like a kid in a candy store, skipping from one to the next?

No such glamour in this brick-lined block of flats for sure – yet it's everywhere you go, isn't it, sex, because sure enough, inside the small hallway affair at the bottom of the stairwell here, in the hidden L-shaped cubbyhole from where the bins are taken out, there's a couple going at it hammer and tongs, right under his nose, real Friday-night behaviour.

Suddenly he's worried: is he witnessing a rape?

With the two lovers and/or rapist-and-his-victim snuffling on the ground there, Larry pauses and wonders what he should do. Earlier in the week he'd read in a newspaper how passers-by had ignored a sex attack in progress thinking it was just mischievous goings-on and he doesn't want to think the same thing could happen again, so he's suddenly astonished to find himself ducking forwards and putting a hand on the man's shoulder and asking over the top of it, Young lady, are you all right?

The girl shouts, Yes! and hides her face quick as a cat; she's strained as hell with the embarrassment and there's a look of white fear on the man's face who's stopped as though switched off at the mains, but nonetheless Larry recognises the girl: Clare, yes, it is, fawn-like little Clare from the third floor – who'd have thought she was that game for it?

Larry is making a dignified exit if that's possible now he's been such a killjoy; but they must admire his bravado, though, to do such a thing and they'd be proud to tell their friends later, we were caught on the job by the Talk Radio DJ and entertainment king, Larry Azure.

Larry might advise Clare, next time he sees her on the staircase which he's presently mounting, that she should spare one of her hands to knead the man's buttocks, hauling and stroking and suchlike expressly to tell all wanderers and passers-by that these are entirely amicable goings-on. Or perhaps a sign painted and hung on the man's back, Fun In Progress.

Reaching the first landing his thoughts are following the same vein – how life is sex through and through – when with a double dose of coincidence Larry sees an old man sitting against the low wall which profiles the block on either side of the closed-off staircases, wanking, shamelessly enjoying himself in full view without a magazine or any other accessory; it doesn't seem like the oldster's concentrating on any imaginary vision of loveliness either because as Larry treads past he's treated to a wink and a friendly nod of the head as the gentleman works away contented as the devil himself, but maybe without much chance of satisfaction if he's being that offhand, but good on him, for having a go.

Then, treading up a further flight of concrete steps and arriving here on the third landing, there's a couple of fifteen-year-olds kissing outside a doorway, but not moronically like people do in the movies, eating each other like ice-cream, instead with true art and delicacy, good kissers both of them. He can hear their murmuring as he climbs the next two flights and good luck to them too, may everyone have great fucks all their lives, he feels like shouting, roll on, make it happen.

Now: in-out, in-out, with the front door key.

As he steps into the flat there's the immediate smell of tonight's cooking and he can hear Grainne's voice; she's on the phone, it must be, because he can't hear anyone else apart from the radio which plays night and day in any case.

Larry stands for a moment and listens.

Yes, she's saying.

Her voice is low-pitched.

She answers the other person, I know, I know but how can I change . . .

He can't make sense of her side of the conversation but it's like she's talking to a lover, it's that emphatic and serious – life-and-death issues only being mulled over by folk who are intimate and his heart sinks at the thought of her having an affair – but he knows she's not, she can't be, she's going out with Larry Azure, she couldn't be wanting an affair.

As he's taking off his coat he hears her say, I have told him.

This means perhaps it's Larry she's talking about.

Ducking into the lounge, he sees her curled up against

4196196

the cushion on the floor, facing away from him, her red hair gathered at the base of her neck and tied with a bright yellow piece of rag, torn and frayed so doubly romantic somehow. Her long black cardigan dress escapes from under the heavily woven jumper and lies in a swathe covering her lower body and she's wearing the black shoes with the funny heels like square blocks flared the wrong way, wider at the bottom than at the top, all the fashion at the moment, but still a delicate enough version of what Larry thinks is a pretty tough shape for ladies' wear, but they suit her, these odd little shoes peeping out at the bottom of her long dress, they make her look like she's living in Dickensian times, or whenever. Certainly she's going to wear them out in no time the way she's going; they're never off her feet.

I know, she's saying emphatically into the phone, I know I shouldn't blame him but I do.

There's an electronic echo which Larry quickly realises is coming from the ghetto-blaster standing on the table next to where he's standing, which is broadcasting her speech; it's like an off-key type of stereo in this room at the moment.

So she's on air.

Larry checks his watch. She's calling the *Milky Way Radio Show*, it must be.

When she's finished, what he'll do is walk up to her and take her by the ears and lift her mouth to his and not say a word; he'll let the occasion ride out by itself carried by the momentum of the whole evening he's passed.

Grainne's looking at him now and holding up an arm which is both a wave hello and an apology for being on the phone and a request for silence during this important time; Larry can see the mascara smeared from her eyes and tears stand on her freckled cheeks, not out of sadness probably, more the excitement mixed with what's obviously a more or less emotional subject matter.

Larry's standing here swaying a touch from side to side and still with the drips of rain coursing down his neck from outside while Grainne's staring at him and meanwhile listening to the telephone headset as Milky the DJ is taking his usual hard line. Over the radio Larry can hear him giving advice, Grainne, blame who you want, all you want, but at the end of the day what's going to change this situation, isn't that what you've got to ask yourself, is it just a case of trying hard enough for long enough, or is it another avenue, a root and branch change?

Now Grainne's talking hard; she might as well be married to Milky Way and the rest of the talk-show DJs, the rate she calls them.

Larry listens as she's saying, But I want to know in advance which is the right path to follow.

This whips him into thinking, Christ, we're all at it, the deciding business.

The radio set replies in a flippant voice, If someone could tell you that, we'd call him God and we'd sit down and pray in front of him, wouldn't we.

I know, Grainne's saying.

Now Milky's getting rid of her quick as he can; he's got

other callers waiting and he's famous for his impatience anyway so he's interrupting her and saying in a dismissive voice, Thanks for calling, Grainne.

Then he's already into his own spiel and Grainne's left holding the phone on her shoulder and biting her lip. I got through, Larry, I was on air.

That's more than exciting, smiles Larry.

Christ, the rain, he adds and lifts his arms like a scarecrow to show how wet he is, turning zombie-like to retreat to the hallway and remove his coat, itself stiffened with water. At the same time he notices the storm has paused for a moment or two; there's not a molecule of air moving. When he came in it was sounding like a kettle whistling sometimes, what with the gusts of wind plucking at the building.

Then he returns to the lounge and notices she's on a different cushion now, out of the five or six with Asian-looking designs scattered around the end of the room in preference to sofas and chairs, all dented from use. She's with her diary, marking down her adventure – the time, the station, the programme, what was said – and he's watching her, the way she holds the pencil.

He can't wait for her to reach the end of her log-book, with what he's dying to tell her.

He asks, So, Grainne, how're you doin'?

She looks up from her writing, watching him for clues.

He persists, grinning at her, You OK?

Fine.

Fit and well?

What's up?

He asks, D'you want to have a fuck, ever?

She's dead still, looking at him like he's offered her something to be wary of.

And what d'you think about the idea of kiddies? he asks.

A look of compassion is crossing her face now and she begins, Larry, you're drunk.

Don't I know that well enough.

So? she asks.

So what d'you think about them as a vague idea, even?

Then she's on her feet with the jumper sleeves trailing over her hands making her look half like a broken ragdoll or puppet and her forehead is crinkling, she's that concerned.

After a while just standing and looking at him like he's an intruder or a suspicious package on an Underground station, she's approaching steadily – a cat on the way closer to a mouse – and she asks, What's happened?

As she arrives nearby Larry takes one of her hands and after uncurling the fingers – intending to hold it against his lips – he's disappointed to have her move on past him to the other side of the room, taking her hand with her.

I've got the wriggler right here, boasts Larry. Loaded, I am, so.

God, he thinks, that's true, that's exactly what he is, loaded, so why's she the other side of the room from him, so far away? If the tadpole which this very minute is waiting in his scrotum can be imagined to have a face, as such, wouldn't it be a frown the poor thing's wearing, worried as to whether the plan's going to stick fast? Larry being on its side wholeheartedly should pray to have the moon at the right spot and the planets lining up, taking Grainne's tides along with them.

The magic tadpole, continues Larry, it's for definite, I'm sure it's putting its goggles on and clapping its hands together like Woody Allen himself.

You're not teasing? she asks him, her eyes darker and wider by the moment as she's suddenly livening up to what's happening here.

Larry swears, No, it's true, and he's a good one, I'm sure of it, as straight as a fucking die with a wiggly tail on him and already dancing away down here; aren't we both hankering to cut ourselves in half, and join up in the middle?

Her face is dead pale as if whitened by chalk like so many redheads, and the freckles will always keep her years younger in appearance. Way over there in the distance, a lonely figure against the wall, she's fastening both her arms around her middle and saying his name like it's a question – Larry? And he knows she's asking, are you sure about all this?

Christ, Grainne, he replies; the loudness in his voice signifies drunkenness or maybe it's just that he cares about this enough to shout from the rooftops, if asked. He wants to go and take her by the hips and start the notorious love-action straight away, why should they be standing like this at opposite ends of the room, isn't it odd, but he knows with her that she'll slither away if he makes a move, it'll backfire and Grainne will be crossed with annoyance just for a second, so all he can do is wave across the abyss and say, I'm telling you here and now to prepare yourself, I'm coming in.

And she's asking directly now, which is unlike her, You sure?

Involuntarily rocking back and forth, which means he's drunk enough nearly to fall over if he does walk towards her – although he can't remember downing that much back at the Dreghorn Castle – he can say, Sure I'm sure.

Suddenly she blows towards him, it looks like that with her willowy walk and the long dress flapping at her ankles, and her hand is now on the side of his face, which unaccountably makes him feel sad, because she feels sorry for him to be making such a gesture.

He says, I am, I know it, because I saw this little scrap of a thing on the way home.

Holding his cheek she asks, What scrap of a thing?

With the rain suddenly arriving again and a new burst of wind rattling the window but the two of them safe in here, Larry is full of himself and answers her, In a manner of speaking, I saw the baby itself, I tell you it was like a vision, kind of, but which stayed there long enough to freak me out, Grainne, I'm telling you, as though it was haunting me.

Grainne is looking doubtful but meanwhile with great care and attention she's touching the area around his mouth as though inspecting a wound for damage while Larry insists – taking his time on account of the suddenly charged atmosphere, the sense of the importance of this encounter, where it might lead to – saying, I was walking along merely and there it was in front of me.

What?

The wee baby-type creature.

So, what was it doing?

Its face and everything was clear as daylight, I tell you it was that odd it had me missing my footing and all, its expression as real as anything, and it was wrapped in a sheet.

When exactly?

On the way home, I saw it, you wouldn't believe, it was an imagination type of thing leading me like a firefly there in the darkness.

And then what, did it speak?

And then it went but I kept on seeing it at five years old and at ten, at sixteen and so on, and it had the freckles, Grainne.

But were you drunk?

What? For me, no I wasn't, but even excusing I was one or two over . . .

She half asks him and half says, You're still drunk, but she's smiling because they've done the alcohol trip often enough together to be conspirators.

In his enthusiasm he carries on, So what is it, d'you think, the opposite of a ghost, when you're visited by the unborn instead of the dead?

I suppose it's still a ghost, she replies.

Well ... whatever. I tell you I saw him clear as day, dancing me home like a wee Pied Piper.

She's not listening but clearing an eye with her wrist, smudging the mascara which still manages to look pretty good, although more Gothic which is at least in keeping with the roll of thunder nearby and the hailstones now clicking against the window sounding like chips frying fills the room with a sense of panic; and all the while she's worming her way into his trousers to coax his cock from its nest and she's rolling it in her hand and looking at it, judging its mystique and general sexual allure as fairly seriously lacking at the moment, no doubt because, he realises, he should be worrying less about the vision he had on the way home and more about his erection shrinking and his balls dropping: his manhood's gone, isn't it, not even kept on the boil by the sight of her very fine breastal developments as they called them when he and his mates were Belfast boys – so Larry can be accused of being too drunk to get it up, like the characters in the newspaper cartoons; added to that is an element of big-match nerves maybe, which doesn't help, failure means something perhaps for the first time in his life.

Larry can't believe the bad luck of having his best ever woman in the flesh, standing right here and half revealed now because she's just slipped off her jersey, lifting it above her head in a scissors movement and not caring for the disarray of the dress underneath revealing more than usual – and she's ready for him and young and warm with all her attractiveness heightened by the flush of success on getting through to the radio show, but ... Christ, soon it will be like when he was a boy coming out of the swimming pool with his cock practically gone from sight, no bigger than a grape hidden in a patch of grass, so he was having to give it a good bashing in the shower afterwards not to feel so undone about it in comparison to the other boys, who were older anyway.

Has the hot water been on tonight, he asks her, because maybe we could give ourselves a bath with the candle standing in the soap dish like before.

Grainne now has the tips of her fingers just bent towards him, and she takes hold of the whole caboodle, the entire package, balls and all. If life was simple, he wonders, what if.

For sure, should it stay like this, his dick a wee pellet, it won't be a good fucking of Grainne that he'll be up to tonight, it'll be the two of them getting the giggles – at best – and probably doom and gloom all round for the wriggler himself, stood down again.

Despite the growl of thunder rolling in – a regular visitor now – Grainne's broken the spell taking her hand away and slapping the side of his hip saying, Shame, eh?

He suggests again, Let's run me a bath and see what can be done to sober me up.

OK.

As they head off for the bathroom Larry's thinking, if this doesn't work then as a last resort he can always think about Laura and picture her in various positions ready and waiting or actually doing it with three men all at once and that nun standing a short distance away, watching and being secretly turned on by it, which might do the trick.

So Laura the serial killer is hurrying up Ben Road towards the estate. The thunder makes her nervous, every clap startles her and she has to stop herself from running to find shelter immediately, anywhere closest by, say in this nook here by the underground station where she might hide and show the whites of her eyes like any other animal; the second break of thunder booms overhead as she's passing the car-wreck-strewn entrance to a garage but still she's managing to hurry past, not ducking in, the danger of such places in themselves goading her on. She is small and worried underneath this careless cracking of energy – lightning – that might kill her if fate says it should, yet here she is as usual walking the last bit whatever the weather so the taxi-drivers won't know where she lives; even in this rain and noise she sticks to her personal security arrangements. She supposes they're the same ones all women have in big cities.

So there's danger all round and from above and inside her even, the test being full on, no way out, that positively against her.

With the lurch of fear at the thought of this fucking world offering no solace from its terrors at all, she recognises she's at her most timid; at times like these she'd do anything anyone told her, even push a knife in someone.

What with the rain and her long coat unbelted and draped over her head in a cowl, she can hope maybe to avoid being followed but she's checking behind her occasionally even so.

She hurries on, her boots skittering through the wet as she turns the corner and steps through the entrance into the estate with its blocks of concrete all looking as though they've blown over in the wind, lying longer than they are tall in a semicircle shape that reminds Laura of a marina in the south of Spain she went to once, the buildings here tethered, it's like, facing into the wind.

In and out of the shadows cast by the streetlights policing this warren of maisonettes, Laura hurries onwards while hearing every now and again a shouting noise and occasionally a shrill whistle from some way off, coming from the area behind the school yard butting on to the railway which is where the youths often hang out, the slope of the embankment giving them enough space to build hides on and they can call it their own day and night, being as well a means to escape from any trouble and filter back on to the streets at various points along its length.

Laura's broken into a trot now, she's having to half-shut her eyes with the discomfort of facing into the more fierce wind and downpour on this side of the first block, hers being the fourth in the semicircle shape.

She could think she's imagining the sound of a voice – where's it coming from now?

When she hears it's a name being called – Michael, Martin? – she wonders if she's really in for it, so she curses. This calling of the stranger's name and the hiss of the rain together gives her the sense she's being swallowed by the bad weather.

She's holding the coat over her head and rounding the corner of block number four which has lost its nameplate, Travers, the sail flapping behind her head and a short distance away a small whirlwind tosses up a polystyrene cup and a crisp packet and last year's leaves, circling uselessly.

Then there's sudden calm, almost on purpose the wind's cancelled at this point to allow her to climb the ramp provided for wheelchairs and so on, access to the raised walkways which skirt the blocks giving on to all the front doors of the maisonettes and she puts on extra speed, suddenly nearly home.

If she can shut the door behind her quick enough she won't have to deal with the outside world any more.

As she gains the walkway she's taken up by the wind again and looking over the side of the parapet she sees below her – as though she's riding in a helicopter looking down to ground level – a stream of kids, male and female, charging up the small alley that leads to a patch of scrub ground between the blocks, shouting, heads not bowed against the rain like hers.

Eerily, there's a flash of lightning which blues the whole

estate but without any accompanying thunder, and Laura has a sudden picture of all three of her wigs standing on polystyrene heads in the bathroom at home which does nothing for her self-esteem, this vision; both that and the crack of thunder arriving now makes her curse, her knees buckling for an instant before she recovers and heads onwards.

Digging in her coat pocket for keys, she's in a panic, having this particular thought: the baby isn't different from the one she killed earlier, it's the same person making a second brave attempt, the cheerful little soul. In her head she apologises, I'm sorry, I know, it's the same situation, I want you I don't want you, I give you a chance and then try and push you back again, I'm sorry, why can't it be straightforward, I'm warped as any killer.

Then she has another thought – look, this warren of homes, whole blocks of them, packed – there must be any number of childless women ticking her off for not putting it up for adoption. God fucking save us from the whole thing, she thinks, the rain pouring on to the pavement at her feet.

Now she's home. The keys fit, the door opens and swings shut behind her.

The weather's gone; suddenly it's quiet and calm and although it's dark and she can hardly see, there are the familiar things which she doesn't have to look out for. This'll be her hiding place. She takes off her coat.

Then she finds herself making a decision: she'll say yes to her sister about the dog. If she's going to cope with the situation she'll need something to hold on to. They can go to Battersea Dogs' Home and find a small terrier or something and they'll have it barking to welcome them home. She'll have to feed it and take it for walks and to the vet for its injections and worming treatments so it'll take her out of herself; she'll have to think about the dog. If not a terrier then a small breed, anyway – it'll be a case of wandering around the cages and seeing something in its eyes saying this is the one.

When her sister comes home or maybe tomorrow morning she'll say yes, she likes the idea after all.

Then, at the exact moment she clicks the light switch on, there comes this shout and a thud against the door she's just closed behind her. It makes her jump.

She calls, Who is it?

Help, comes a child's voice.

After a moment thinking about safety, she opens the door. A lad is standing there with a small dog on a piece of string, a terrier-cross, which takes her breath away.

It leaps to mind – this is the sign, the dog she wanted. It's a beige, short-haired animal with perhaps some poodle in it as well.

She hasn't seen this boy before. He's dark but with very white skin and staring eyes. As she stands in the doorway the kid bursts into tears and waves his arms. The string jerks the dog's neck. The dog moves closer with a hop. Laura sees that one of its rear legs is injured; there's a rag wrapped around it.

She asks, What's the matter?

The boy doesn't answer; he just has this begging look and she can see tears. She knows he's fooling her.

Come on, tell me.

The boy stoops and rubs his leg. Christ, he shouts, someone stabbed me up.

He hops once or twice.

Christ.

Her hand's on the door; she could still close it if she wanted to.

She asks, Have you hurt your leg?

The boy doesn't answer but his face is a mask of pain. He holds out both arms; the string tied to the dog is still in his hand.

Let's have the dog off you, any road.

Laura holds the lead and at the same time takes the boy's hand. How could he be looking after it properly? She'll need to take it to the vet's.

She says to the boy, You can tell me, can't you, what's wrong.

He says angrily, Someone got to me and tried to stab me up, didn't they, and I ran away and fell, jumping off the roof.

It's a prank, she tells herself, don't be an idiot. She knows she ought to shut the door on the boy even with the rain and the wind – but there's the dog.

He's holding on to both her hands. The dog's in the flat now standing on three legs and looking around like it's deciding whether or not to move in. Every time its lead shortens it walks a pace or two, because Laura's walking backwards, the boy limping, using her like a walking frame. She looks beyond him to see if any of the other kids are waiting.

She asks, What's your name?

In the hallway the boy drops and sits on the carpet with one leg straight in front of him. He's pleading with her and rubbing his leg. She thinks maybe he's Polish or from Eastern Europe somewhere. He's not stopped staring at her face with his questioning look.

Where on your leg does it hurt?

She goes to help him but he screams and shrinks from her, bending over his body to protect it as if to say leave him right there. But she knows he's lying, she can sense it, the same as when they come round saying they're collecting for charity.

I need a doctor, man!

Laura puts her hands on her hips, trying to decide what to do.

The dog is whining, holding its bandaged leg off the ground. The boy is rocking back and forth, moaning. She decides to phone for someone anyway, maybe not the police or ambulance, it isn't an emergency; the doctor should be enough, then she'll have time to cancel when the boy runs off with her purse or whatever he's up to.

As she goes to the living room to phone her GP, she's thinking of this life she could have had. Doctor, my child's hurt himself, she imagines saying.

She's not let any of the kids inside before now. This is the first and last time. She could have a good cry herself.

When all this is sorted out she'll lie down on the sofa and crash out. She'll think about Larry some more. Maybe her sister will come home.

She gives instructions to the doctor's night service. Now there'll be a delay and some more bother before it's cleared up.

By the time she's finished giving her address and number and put the phone down, it's gone quiet in the hallway. Is the child dead? she wonders. Does she remember her life-saving class? She steps back into the hallway.

When she sees him, the boy's on his feet. There's a video recorder under his arm which is causing him trouble, he's struggling to balance it. Both the boy and the dog pause, and look at her. The brat is robbing her.

Something inside her falls – that's the sensation – and whatever it is, her pride or dignity, hurts.

The boy frees one hand from the machine to wrap the string twice round his fingers and give the dog a tug. He's balancing the recorder on his knees and then he's trying to turn and run out of the front door. He can't do it, his balance isn't there so he puts the recorder down and tries picking it up again. He's in a hurry to get out and she supposes she should let him go, but with or without the video recorder? Through the door to her bedroom she can see the wires trailing from the console opposite the divan. Her TV is lying on its side; it was probably too heavy.

He's swearing and kicking at the door, Fuck, come on, you fuck, open, you fuck.

Laura feels bad. It's like the kid is acting out a scene

from a video – and here he is stealing the machine to play it on. Now he's wrestling with the door catch, the dog being pulled by the neck on its piece of string. When the boy gets the door open and stoops to pick up the recorder the dog is suddenly free to turn and look at her balefully.

She takes two paces towards him and says, Bring it back when you've finished with it.

She hears her own words and is guilty. Why doesn't she just take the machine off him? The answer is, she doesn't want the kid to have stolen it so she's making out it's a loan and she's agreed – yes, he can borrow it for a while. More than that, she's scared.

The boy isn't taking any notice of her. He's still playing his scene. Now the door's open and he's on the run down the walkway. The string whips tight on the dog's neck, which makes it sit on its backside and refuse to move. The kid ploughs on, dragging the dog. Laura's heart jumps at the cruelty. The dog still doesn't get up even as the boy gathers pace. It deliberately drops on to its side and sleighs off like that with its bandaged leg in the air.

Laura shouts, Oi!

She's outraged but can't think what to do.

She waits up for an hour, pacing back and forth forgetting where she is, who she is or what she can do at all beyond clearing up where the kid walked off with the video; she was hoping to catch her sister coming in but now she gives up on her, whereupon she goes through the usual routine, posting the wig on its stand next to the other two in the bathroom and cleaning her teeth and dunking her

face in hot water for some minutes before patting it dry
and falling into bed where for a minute or two she touches
her scalp to find out if her hair is growing back, measuring
the tufts by teasing them in her fingers.

Next door's television switches off; in the quiet she wonders about all the other flats and houses around her, what
cruelties there are that people are suffering at the same
time as her.

Eventually, she falls asleep.

Now she's dreaming – she can see what looks like an
insect pinned to a board for a school biology experiment –
a finger is pointing – but moving closer she's alarmed to
see it's herself in miniature, spread-eagled and pinned by
the wrists and ankles, with the tip of the person's finger
touching her gently on the chest and abdomen. There's a
voice; she can't make out the words but from the tone she
guesses it's a teacher or lecturer – a man – explaining
something to onlookers. The finger presses harder and she
feels a rising panic: whoever it is thinks she's dead, it's a
mistake but there's no one on her side to say stop, look
she's alive, the formaldehyde didn't work, you can see her
moving. The odds are stacked against her, she'll have to
fight harder, to shout.

The finger is trembling and out of focus as it points first
here, then in different places while the emphasis in the
voice switches, becomes keener and now she sees the finger
is delicately picking at her middle, to lift a flap of flesh that
will reveal her internal organs. She can see her own face
and she realises no one will guess she's conscious because

her head is tilted back with the mouth open and the lips falling inwards around the edges like an old person's, her eyes not just shut but giving off that sense they won't open again, and her worst thought is, this is her ugliest, without hair, the eyes closed and her mouth gaping like she is dead – no one will want to save her. This is it.

With the teacher's finger holding open the cut in her middle, a metal instrument appears from the other side, it looks like the prong dentists use to scrape away plaque. As the tip descends the voice stops – the last phrase hangs in the air like a question and what's to happen next will be the answer. She is seized with terror watching the steel tip go into her but there's no pain, although the sensation of it moving is like a worm in her middle, stirring. She's transfixed, then, watching the instrument catch at a membrane and peel it back like the skin on boiled milk – because there's no blood, only this whitish film. The voice starts up again, more excited now and both the finger holding back the flesh and the instrument itself are shaking with nerves. It's a struggle for her to see; it's as though she has to lean closer, but so do the other students watching, so there isn't the room for all their heads to fit this close – although she can't see them this is the sense she has, that she's part of the crowd being taught. Pushing forwards she has this sudden sickness because she can see what looks like a nest of baby mice, pink and hairless, eyes tightly shut; this is what they've been looking for all along, what the voice is excited about and what the students have gathered to watch.

The metal probe dips in and touches one of the baby mice – *dab* – and she feels it as a thread of pain drawn from her navel and worse comes when she sees the pink, unformed creature, still alive, hanging from the tip of metal as it withdraws – then it's gone and she senses the shake of the teacher's arm as he gets rid of it.

It happens again and again; each time there's the sense of a pain being drawn from her and the blind unknow-ingness of whatever creature it is being taken from its nest, described by the kindly voice of the teacher.

Then the metal instrument withdraws and in its place appears a thin glass tube; she recognises it's a pipette which steadies just above her, a drip appearing on the end of it. Seeing this bead of liquid wobbling precariously on the nose of the instrument, panic yawns in her; she knows that if it drops, she'll die.

From her viewpoint she tries to tell whoever's in control to stop but there's no voice available to her, so how can she persuade everyone watching that she has the whole story, she can see it from both angles, inside and out, whereas the people observing only notice that she's not quite dead and this is something that needs to be done.

The drop of liquid fills her mind's eye, it's all she can see; its refractions shaking with the movement, the tension filling as it becomes larger, gathering volume and then suddenly it's coming towards her and she has this sensation of a hand pushing her over the edge so now she'll always be falling, there's nothing else but to accelerate into a depth that won't bottom out but will be a constant, living terror, and there are others all around her in the same predicament; as she calls out, the sound of her voice is what's summoning her from sleep – and she's awake and sitting upright.

Larry, calls Grainne, you can open your eyes now.

With his hand on this fucking Eiffel Tower of an erection Larry Azure is lying on the bed, his eyes closed, holding the shaft vertical for maximum pride.

He can imagine the future Larry Azure, international entertainment star, stripped across the week in primetime radio and TV, leaning back in his chair and putting his hands behind his head and not worrying about the length of the pause – his audiences will love the silence, waiting for it to happen, listening to him breathing like this, no more needed, and when he finally does talk via the microphone into the darkness he knows x million listeners will be hanging off his every word and he'd begin, Ladies and gentlemen . . .

Then he'd give them maybe another wait, a few in-out breaths and a sigh to show people he's thinking all right and it'd be worth it, to hang on for a second or two because by then the audience loyalty would be like rock-solid, no fucking manager or scheduler would be able to touch him with their compulsory fucking playlists and he could have them on the edges of their seats while he sits in his studio with the photographs of all the stars he's had visit him pinned to the walls with the personal messages scrawled across them – because he, Larry, is saying something the audience will recognise and want to hear about, bang on true, they'd eat it up, even the studio technicians would put down their biscuits and stop sipping tea in order to watch him through the glass, all of them in absolute, gold-plated awe as he says, Ladies and gentlemen, I was standing with my girlfriend in the bedroom of our penthouse apart-ment overlooking the park with the cars streaming by beneath my feet and the jets queuing in the sky above our heads and despite the rain and the howling wind and the tense situation there happened to be existing between us at that moment, I came up behind her and put my hand on her stomach and I thought, what a machine is in there, for breeding purposes. A woman's body is the miracle – forget water into wine which in comparison is a dry piece of bread all right. Put a girl and a boy in the same room and the whole point to the sex game is, there should be this reproductive thing, ladies and gentlemen, between us, isn't that true? But the result is, you might say, as those of us who've had a few children already will know, bloody. It's blood and guts and the slaughterhouse of life as a fellow once said.

Then, he hears his name, Larry . . .

He lifts himself on to his elbows to see what Grainne's decided on for the occasion.

She's standing there – undressed to kill as Larry once read in a magazine – her arms outstretched and her gaze steadily heavenwards in the mock-angelic pose she does,

with his favourite salmon-pink gown laced up ever so gin-
gerly down her front, the silk cord hopefully like those you
get on the economy packs of dogfood which if you know
how to tease the bit of string just so, the stitching across
the top unravels suddenly as if by magic. He knows that
beneath the gown she'll have the one-piece on, made out
of perforated black lace with a swimsuit cut and undoing,
he remembers very well, via the two delicate press-studs
located between her legs, if he wants to take it off at all.

Larry wonders, is his head spinning from the sight of
her or from the booze, still.

Grainne, come here.

He's looking on in dismay because as he might have
known she's turned and flitted from the room; it's not for
her, is it, the schmaltzy walk towards him and the laying
on of hands and the pouting lips – you're talking about
someone who the most you hear of her is when she's in
another room singing to herself, or that wild shriek and
cursing she gives when she sees something she doesn't like
in the bathroom mirror. No, the game is, Larry has a chase
on his hands here.

He ups from the bed and feels the blood drain from his
skull, which gives him this moronic walk to the door, shaking his head; by the time he's looking down the first part
of the L-shaped hallway she's facing him at the other end,
her palms turned back, flat against the wall; she's waiting.
His dizziness clears.

She asks – as though she's never seen him before – Who
are you?

Casting himself in one of her favourite fantasies here for
a moment Larry says, I'm a big black motherfucker of a
basketball player.

You're not, so.

All right I'm a singer-entertainer and all-round diamond
guy with black curly hair and I used to have an American
car you once liked going in.

I remember, too, driving in that car of yours.

Meanwhile Larry's catching up with her but then she's
spinning like a top, the gown flaring like a dancer's and
she's disappeared.

Grainne, calls Larry and he advances to the elbow of the
corridor here, guessing which of the rooms she's gone in.
There are three closed doors to choose from.

Will it be the lounge, most likely?

With his hand on the door-lever sudden memories come
to him of the times they've ended up doing the business in
here. As the cushions take up most of the space they've
usually featured, either doubling for a bed or as a wedge
for her to be half-on, half-off or as bolsters of one type or
another; they might have been designed for it and sold in
the sex shops, love pods.

Grainne? he asks, opening the door very slowly, inch by
inch, so playing the hunter all right and topping up the
erotic play of events here with a quick thought of Laura –
a girl he used to know, didn't she work in a pub or something – with her bare ass in the air criss-crossed with
the usual suspenders-and-stockings arrangement and her
forehead knocking with a dull *thunk* against the floor tiles

in an old toilet . . . Anyways, well done, you cock, he's
inwardly saying while holding the massive stick in front of
him, not bad for a drunk, but don't you let me down now
by falling asleep on the job; Christ, he swears, if you do
I'll never talk to you again, you lazy gun – is it because
you're shamed, guilty at the terrible tricks you've played
on people so a touch reluctant to show your head above
the parapet? Whichever's the case forget it, Larry orders,
you're on for the proper thing tonight, for the sake of God
keep your blood up and get on with it, stay this hard.

But the lounge is empty. The cushions are plain old
cushions, not the romping ground for the conception of
his first-born after all.

A disappointed man, Larry turns on his heel and stops
dead, listening. Sometimes she gives him a clue: a snatch
of a song or a signal, like the bathroom taps suddenly
running.

Only there's silence, so she's making it difficult.

Next Larry tries the kitchen, the most unlikely place but
the occasional knee-trembler has been achieved in here
with Grainne cornered usually partly dressed but speared
all right and her feet off the ground with the excitement,
or leaning face-down on the little breakfast table with their
in-out action moving the whole assembly – Grainne and
the table and everything – steadily across the floor.

Following his cock he adds a handful of fuel to the fire:
remembering the way an ex-girlfriend – Patty, he thinks
her name was – lifted her hands and held her own breasts

together to make a deeper cleavage for him to use as he wanted.

But it's a neat and tidy workable little room with no sign of his very own pet temptress and mother-to-be of their first child anywhere to be seen.

She's not in the lounge or the kitchen, which means, odds-on, that he's up for a go in the spare room because he remembers he used all the hot water already taking a bath just now so there can't be the water-sports option – the spare room's the only one left.

He tiptoes to the door and stands for a while listening, but hears nothing. Remembering another of her fantasies he taps his knuckles against the plywood and introduces himself, calling, Pizza delivery boy.

He waits, but there's nothing. He adds, Dressed in leathers.

Silence.

The time or two they've ended up in here before has been like rampaging through a garbage depot what with the bags full of stuff, the old blankets, broken hoovers and the cardboard boxes full of God knows what which they've never unpacked thrown in, so they ended up all anyhow themselves in the pile of rubbish, the interesting thing being what ended up printed on their skins from the pushing and the shoving and general friction; once he remembers she had this neat squared pattern across her arse like you see on a flame-grilled burger, from some netting lying about it was, God knows.

Larry listens at the door but there's silence; still, he's certain she's in there.

This is it, Larry, brace yourself and hope it happens.

Is his mouth drying up completely?

Larry holds his breath and goes in, but this isn't the spare room at all: what greets him first is the candlelight thrown by a single flame in the middle of the floor.

The next instant he marks a sudden sense of space like he's walked to the edge of a cliff because he can see to the edges of the room – the floor is clear of the usual debris and the walls are as bare as when they moved in. So facing him is this blank room – except for Grainne lying there on the duvet in a picturesque Z-shape shrouded by her gown, the candle standing on the floor a short distance off for safety's sake, its flame guttering in the little scented jar because of the breeze caused by his opening the door just now.

Where's all the stuff, he wonders, squashed into the cupboards in here or thrown out in dustbin bags? It must have been when he was taking his bath that she cleared up the place and put down the spare duvet on the carpet and borrowed the candle from the lounge, Larry guesses.

She's not moved a muscle or said anything.

He takes a step into the room, calling her name, Grainne.

She doesn't react but stays motionless, her eyes closed as though asleep.

He doesn't want to hope too much, but are they on for one of his favourite games, playing dead?

He kneels and touches her hip, rolling it back and forth.

Then he strokes her arm and asks in a low, keen voice, Is
Grainne dead as a doornail, maybe?

There's no response so Larry knows that whatever he
says or does to her from now on, the form is, she'll be a
lifeless dummy until after he's shot his load – and from
previous experience, it's true, she'll be as committed to it
as a top actress playing the death scene in a movie. If he
makes a joke she won't laugh, if he drags her about and
ties her limbs to the four corners of the room she won't
flinch or tighten a muscle even; whether or not he takes
his time or goes at it like a bull in a china shop she won't
murmur a word of encouragement or complaint but stay
loose as a corpse. Only if she comes before he does will
she suddenly give the game away with her two or three
short moans, but he won't be far behind, the noise she
makes being so torn from her – because of her biting back
on it that much – it's usually enough of a spur to take him
over the edge, anyway.

As he idly takes the pencil-thin straps of her gown and
lifts them from her shoulders so he can work towards
freeing her breasts from the one-piece, he thinks what a
vision, this pink gown floating on the cloud-like duvet, lit
by the candle, on the floor with her red hair loose like she's
drowned, it's a picture all right.

Suddenly it hits him what it means, the room cleared
like this and it's typical of her to send a message in such a
roundabout way, for him to work it out rather than have it
handed to him on a plate. What she's saying to him loud
and clear is, You know that baby you saw, Larry, Pied-

Pipering you home, well this is its room, where it'll be put down to sleep; its little in-out breaths will be bringing a puff of life to in here so let's start off where we mean to go on with it, do it here inside these four walls, come on, it's where the beginning of the story should be.

At the same time he understands why exactly she's saying let's me play dead, because they're up to the opposite, aren't they, sponsoring a life, so the irony of it slaps him full in the face: deep in her insides the game of creation's to be kicked off here tonight after which point it'll run way out of their control, the same way since Adam first jumped Eve – but a perfect grace stroke all right is what it's going to be, this fuck, for Christ's sake.

Larry puts a hand on her hip and thinks how, like, dish-shaped it is compared to a man's because of the work it's to do, what it's to serve up, you might say, which is to be put in motion right now, they're cooking tonight, and his hand's gathering the pink viscose material which glimmers at him in the candlelight revealing her shank white as anything and then he's rolling her on to her back, a dead weight with a stream of ginger hair covering most of her face and her arm flopping sideways so he lifts the gown higher to see the black lacework underwear which they call skimpy in the magazines, and her cleavage is there, the vertical smile he can enjoy 'til he's in his grave for sure – how come it has that power over him, *thy two breasts are like two young roes which are twins* – and he's leaning over her to breathe in the smell and cruise over the whole landscape like he's in a helicopter gunship, missiles bursting all right, to let go.

He lands between her breasts and slavers over both mounds with no response from her; she's an expert all right and it's OK to know she's posting herself off to a dream world herself no matter what he's doing, she's imagining the gang of schoolboys entering her every which way with their cocks small and quick but plentiful like Chinese food or the basketball player pulling out the big one and scoring against her, so he, Larry, can do what he wants and think what he likes in isolation, but also in perfect communion with her, which is what's brilliant.

He has both his hands wrapped around her breasts and her legs are askew and her personality switched off and his favourite woman is like this beckoning him to the ultimate, a fuck without contraception in the hope of springing a person that's half him, half her made somehow out of the excitement between them; the urge to get on and do it is uncoiling in the bottom of his groin.

So, the singer-entertainer-barman Larry Azure is making love with his wife like a gentleman, moving slowly to and fro, *the joints of thy thighs are like jewels*, closing his eyes now after noting the rain beating against the window and holding as a picture to turn him on Grainne's pink gown tight over her breasts, and he's glad to have arrived, to be doing it, his cock a swollen shaft here, pinning him to his wife who's lying dead still but warm with her heart beating away inside her, so loud he can almost hear it, or is it his own? Whichever, it's the hunting ground for his firstborn he's moving into and with each tilt forwards he's walking two or three miles, you might say, into the wilderness that Larry imagines surrounds the mystery of God's creation, and each pull backwards is only to recharge, ready to accelerate forwards by as much again, the excitement, the rush, loading in his cock piece by piece, an achievement in itself, until there'll be the overfill – and his ambition is to have such an orgasm that will unlock the gates all right, *the kingdom of heaven is at hand.*

He's that charged up, though, that it might happen too quickly at this rate; suddenly it's not three miles he's advancing but hundreds at a time and the edge he's to fall over is right there in front of him and since he's maybe never again to have this moment he ought to savour it for a touch longer so the imaginary cry to himself is, Wait, you bastard, hang on. The delay spray he's seen advertised in magazines is what's needed but the only trick he knows is to think of something dull as ditchwater, as far away from sex as possible – and by accident it's old, blind Tom, leaning forward to dabble his fingers in the ashtray, which comes to mind.

Christ, the desire's in him like a lead weight, though, pinning a load of happiness in his groin; this is the life, the unadulterated life pure and simple going about its business of making more life, the same as in every other bedroom throughout the whole history of the men shafting the women; perfect it is as well to hear right now a crash of thunder so loud it shakes the window and bangs in his lungs, the noise is that great, the work of God, and now

for a truly boring and un-erotic picture in his mind to help
him hold off from coming, he takes to thinking of the very
stern and humourless face, a portrait of Jesus his ma asked
him to kiss every night before going to bed – but wouldn't
it be like father like son, surely the old Daddy Greybeard
himself must have an ounce more humour in him than
Larry's ma signalled, certainly, to have thought up this trick
for rolling his creation forwards in time all right, and a
warm heart to share it out to everyone wholesale, practically, not to mention including this thunder-and-lightning
show for Larry Azure, free of charge.

To switch off even more urgently from the sight of
Grainne's magic triangle here beneath him where her two
legs and the waist come together to offer him the whole
of her sex with its shadowy entrance and her navel there
like a round goblet which wanteth not liquor, Larry pictures a
queue of bald monks wearing hair shirts and washing
muddy vegetables, just to allow him a minute or two more,
please, of this stumbling run he's taking through the garden
of Eden, for Christ's sake; and Larry Azure finds he's
inwardly talking, saying whatever or whoever you are, God,
thanks for this, take a pat on the back, you did OK, and if
it's what you meant all along by that famous phrase of
yours, baptism by desire, here I am, I've arrived, haven't I,
one of your people – I can't believe this isn't what you
meant.

Just then he hears Grainne catch her breath and he opens
his eyes to such a sight, her holding her lip in her teeth
and moving the hand resting on her belly just slightly

downwards while her legs are still collapsed one on each side of him, milky white in the candlelight while her hair is flaming red, and he knows this slight movement betraying the fact she's alive means she's standing on the same edge as he is so there's no need to think of anything, just stroke them both over and fall together hopefully, which would be a signal all right of good luck and so he's racing a little now with the thought of it, *let your loins be girded about and your lights burning*, watching her mouth open a touch more and her neck stretch fractionally and the blush rising upwards from her chest like a wave of blood he ought to go with himself; he's riding it and it carries them along; helpless things they are, done for.

LOUIS DE BERNIÈRES
Captain Corelli's Mandolin

In war-torn Cephallonia a young Italian, Captain Antonio Corelli, is left in charge of the occupying troops. At first he is ostracised by the locals, but as a conscientious but far from fanatical soldier, whose main aim is to have a peaceful war, he proves in time to be civilised, humorous – and a consummate musician.

When the local Doctor's daughter's letters to her fiancé – and members of the underground – go unanswered, the working of the eternal triangle seems inevitable. But can this fragile love survive as a war of bestial savagery gets closer and the lines are drawn between invader and defender?

'*Captain Corelli's Mandolin* is an emotional, funny, stunning novel which swings with wide smoothness between joy and bleakness, personal lives and history . . . it's lyrical and angry, satirical and earnest'

Observer

'Louis de Bernières is in the direct line that runs through Dickens and Evelyn Waugh . . . he has only to look into his world, one senses, for it to rush into reality, colours and touch and taste'

A. S. Byatt, *Evening Standard*

'*Captain Corelli's Mandolin* is a wonderful, hypnotic novel of fabulous scope and tremendous iridescent charm – and you can quote me'

Joseph Heller

'A true diamond of a novel, glinting with comedy and tragedy'

Daily Mail

GORDON BURN

Fullalove

Norman Miller used to be one of Fleet Street's finest. Now he's a middle-aged, burned-out hack with a gift for the sensational story, the shouting tabloid lead. But as he reports on a series of brutal murders and sex crimes, he's forced to wonder whether he is just a witness – or part of some deeper pattern of cause and effect . . .

'Remarkable . . . devastating . . . required reading for anyone interested in what British fiction should be doing today'
Stephen Amidon, *Esquire*

'Startling, memorable . . . blackly and brilliantly painted . . . If there is anyone out there who feels complacent about the way we live now, Gordon Burn's novel will disabuse them'
Victoria Glendinning, *Daily Telegraph*

'A rich and awesome work . . . intensely, almost fatiguingly brilliant . . . With it, Burn establishes himself as British fiction's leading specialist in the scuzzy aspects of contemporary life'
Phil Baker, *Times Literary Supplement*

'Extraordinary . . . A shriek of hyper-literate rage . . . One of the year's most richly imagined and provocative novels'
Boyd Tonkin, *New Statesman & Society*

'Brilliant . . . the writing is consistently superb, burning with a hard, gem-like intensity'
Steve Grant, *Time Out*

ALISON HABENS

Dreamhouse

Celia Small has been planning her engagement party for years. Now the big day has arrived, her best fantasy is about to come true.

But two of her hated housemates are also having parties tonight, and their impromptu affairs are quite at odds with Celia's prim, family arrangements. With three parties in one house, Celia is set for the worst night of her life.

Led astray by a drug-dealing White Rabbit and a trail of dodgy jam tarts, Celia wanders like an accidental Alice into a weird Wonderland of drugs and dressing-up, psychedelia and social deviance, on a one-way trip of self-discovery.

'One of the best first novels to appear this year'

Sunday Times

'A truly astonishing feat of the imagination, supported by a dazzling display of wit and wordplay'

Sunday Times

'Curious and magical . . . Alison Habens has a refreshingly playful love of language, and is endlessly inventive'

The Times

'Like Carroll, Habens has a talent for playfulness so deft that it conceals its craft'

Independent on Sunday

SAM NORTH

Chapel Street

**A brilliantly powerful novel of the nature of time,
sexual relationships and change**

'A decaying London house, a crazy landlady, a motley and
cosmopolitan crew of tenants trying to sort out their lives and
tangled loves: this is symbolist's terrain and Sam North aims high.
His writing is crisp, observant and very funny'

Independent on Sunday

'A radiant piece of writing'

Observer

'The residents of Chapel Street are the product of a humorous and
inventive mind. Dickens crossed with Pinter might spawn
something similar, but they cue most to reality . . . North is a not
a lyricist. His spare, conversational prose wastes no time and takes
no prisoners . . . *Chapel Street* has the verve of a cult novel and the
confident form of a mature work. Sam North's is an intriguing
talent'

Scotland on Sunday

'*Chapel Street* adds grace and muscle to the sinewy agility of his
earlier [Somerset Maugham Award] prizewinner *The Automatic
Man*'

Jonathan Keates, *Independent*

SAM NORTH

The Gifting Programme

**A haunting, moving story of inheritance, greed
and loneliness by the prizewinning author of
*The Automatic Man***

'Amberlin Sayers is an American myth, lost at the centre of his
self-made fortune. Getting old, without family or friends, he
summons three people from the past and offers to divide his
corporation between them, in exchange for some shared memories
and company . . . North uses charged prose – tackling great
obstacles, great changes, great epiphanies at every turn'

Time Out

'*The Gifting Programme* is mannered, deliberate, fabulous in more
ways than one . . . and what grips is the detailed precision, the
intricacies that North invests in his cast of modern Americans, the
baggage they carry, the disparate worlds they inhabit'

Independent

'A buoyant, intelligent work, beautifully wrought, and sparkling
with stylistic panache'

The Times

A Selected List of Fiction Available from Minerva

While every effort is made to keep prices low, it is sometimes necessary to increase prices at short notice Mandarin Paperbacks reserves the right to show new retail prices on covers which may differ from those previously advertised in the text or elsewhere.

The prices shown below were correct at the time of going to press.

☐	7493 9754 3	**Captain Corelli's Mandolin**	Louis de Bernières	£6.99
☐	7493 9962 7	**Señor Vivo and the Coca Lord**	Louis de Bernières	£6.99
☐	7493 9857 4	**The Troublesome Offspring of Cardinal Guzman**	Louis de Bernières	£6.99
☐	7493 9130 8	**The War of Don Emmanuel's Nether Parts**	Louis de Bernières	£6.99
☐	7493 8638 X	**Fullalove**	Gordon Burn	£6.99
☐	7493 9056 5	**Nothing Natural**	Jenny Diski	£6.99
☐	7493 9960 0	**Trick or Treat**	Lesley Glaister	£4.99
☐	7493 1766 3	**Dreamhouse**	Alison Habens	£6.99
☐	7493 9883 3	**How late it was, how late**	James Kelman	£6.99
☐	7493 9714 4	**The Lights Below**	Carl MacDougall	£5.99
☐	7493 9090 5	**Stone Over Water**	Carl MacDougall	£6.99
☐	7493 9112 X	**Hopeful Monsters**	Nicholas Mosley	£7.99
☐	7493 9876 0	**Chapel Street**	Sam North	£5.99
☐	7493 9875 2	**The Gifting Programme**	Sam North	£5.99
☐	7493 9618 0	**Shear**	Tim Parks	£5.99
☐	7493 9622 9	**Still**	Adam Hope	£6.99
☐	7493 9704 7	**Ulverton**	Adam Hope	£5.99
☐	7493 9747 0	**Swing Hammer Swing**	Jeff Torrington	£5.99
☐	7493 9134 0	**Rebuilding Coventry**	Sue Townsend	£5.99

All these books are available at your bookshop or newsagent, or can be ordered direct from the address below. Just tick the titles you want and fill in the form below.

Cash Sales Department, PO Box 5, Rushden, Northants NN10 6YX.
Phone: 01933 414000 : Fax: 01933 414047.

Please send cheque, payable to 'Reed Book Services Ltd.', or postal order for purchase price quoted and allow the following for postage and packing:

£1.00 for the first book, 50p for the second; **FREE POSTAGE AND PACKING FOR THREE BOOKS OR MORE PER ORDER.**

NAME (Block letters) ....

ADDRESS...

....

☐ I enclose my remittance for...........................

☐ I wish to pay by Access/Visa Card Number

Expiry Date

Signature . . . .

Please quote our reference: MAND